Archie Greene
and the
Alchemists' Curse

ALSO BY D. D. EVEREST

Archie Greene and the Magician's Secret

Archie Greene
and the
Alchemists' Curse

D. D. Everest

HARPER
An Imprint of HarperCollinsPublishers

Archie Greene and the Alchemists' Curse
Copyright © 2016 by D. D. Everest
All rights reserved. Printed in the United States of America.
No part of this book may be used or reproduced in any manner
whatsoever without written permission except in the case of brief quotations
embodied in critical articles and reviews. For information address
HarperCollins Children's Books, a division of HarperCollins Publishers,
195 Broadway, New York, NY 10007.
www.harpercollinschildrens.com

ISBN 978-0-06-231214-3 (trade bdg.)

Typography by Carla Weise
16 17 18 19 20   CG/RRDH   10 9 8 7 6 5 4 3 2 1
❖
First U.S. edition, 2016. Published in the U.K. by Faber and Faber in 2016.

For Lindsay, lunch companion and woods trotter extraordinaire.
And for our father, Peter Dearlove, who would have loved to have seen it.

Contents

Inside the Museum of Magical Miscellany, a dust sheet covered an ancient wooden plaque on the wall. Written on it were the names of the five most gifted and notorious apprentices of all time.

The Alchemists' Club, founded 1662
Fabian Grey
Braxton Foxe
Felicia Nightshade
Angelica Ripley
Roderick Trevallen

The Lores of Magical Restraint

In 1666, half of London was consumed in the Great Fire, which started in the cellar of a baker's shop in Pudding Lane and was caused by a magical accident. To avoid a panic among the people of London, the royal baker, Thomas Farrinor, was blamed (and that is the version of history that is still taught to children in Unready schools). But the English king, Charles II, knew that a reckless magical experiment started the fire. At his insistence, steps were taken to prevent another magical disaster.

From that day forward, magicians had to practice magic according to a set of strict rules known as the Lores of Magical Restraint. The Lores were intended as a temporary measure, but they remain in force to this day. Many people in the magical realm believe the Lores should be lifted and magic practiced openly once more, but the governing bodies of magic continue to resist these calls.

FIRST LORE: All magical books and artifacts must be returned to the Museum of Magical Miscellany for inspection and classification. (They are classified as level one, two, or three in magical power.)

SECOND LORE: Magical books and artifacts may not be used or bought and sold until properly identified and classified.

THIRD LORE: The unauthorized use of magic outside of magical premises is prohibited.

FOURTH LORE: The hoarding of magical books and artifacts to accumulate personal power is outlored under the prohibition of dangerous practices.

FIFTH LORE: The mistreatment of magical creatures is expressly forbidden.

CHAPTER 1

The Vanishing Fruitcake

On the roof of the Bodleian Library in Oxford, a raven sat so still that it appeared to be carved from stone. Its flinty black eyes observed a boy as he passed below. The boy's name was Archie Greene.

At that moment, Archie felt a prickling, tickling sensation in the palm of his right hand. He glanced at the small tattoo-like mark there in the shape of a needle and thread. It was the Firemark he'd received when he started his apprenticeship as a magical bookbinder. Normally, it didn't bother him, but today it was itching.

Archie was twelve and small for his age, with spiky brown hair, but otherwise looked perfectly normal. The

1

only clue that there was anything out of the ordinary about him, apart from the Firemark on his hand, was the color of his eyes. One was emerald green and the other was silvery gray—a sign of magical ability.

It was the end of the summer holidays and Oxford was teeming with parents buying school uniforms for their children. Not having a mother or father of his own, Archie couldn't help but watch with curiosity.

Glancing up the high street, Archie saw another telltale sign—a girl with pigtails emerged from a stationery shop clutching a new pencil case. It was nearly time to go back to school, and in the past Archie would've been shopping for cheap secondhand uniforms with his gran.

But not this year! At the beginning of the summer everything had changed for Archie. He had discovered cousins he never knew existed, and he had found out that he was descended from the Flame Keepers of Alexandria, a secret community devoted to finding and preserving magical books.

This term Archie would be receiving a very different sort of schooling—as an apprentice at the Museum of Magical Miscellany. The museum was Oxford's best-kept secret. It was hidden beneath the Bodleian Library.

Over the summer, Old Zeb, the museum's bookbinder, had been teaching Archie how to repair magical books.

With the start of the new term, Archie would be learning more advanced Bookbinding, including how to cast spells. Then, when he received his next Firemark, he'd start one of the other two magical apprenticeships—Finding or Minding.

Magical books fascinated Archie. Gran had always said that books were in his blood, and over the summer he'd found out why. Since starting his apprenticeship he had discovered a very rare talent: he was a book whisperer, which meant he could talk to magical books.

Archie didn't understand how book whispering worked or what he was supposed to do with his unusual ability. But he loved being an apprentice at the museum—surrounded by books and friends.

"Why are you looking so pleased with yourself?" asked Bramble Foxe, one of Archie's cousins, who had stopped to look in a shop window with him. Bramble was nearly fifteen, with green eyes and long, dark, curly hair. She was on her second apprentice skill at the museum, as a Minder, having completed her training as a Finder and received her second Firemark.

"I was just thinking about everything that's happened since I came to Oxford," he said, grinning. And a lot had happened.

A magical book he had been sent on his twelfth

birthday had turned out to be *The Book of Souls*, a book of dark magic written by a warlock called Barzak. It was one of the Terrible Tomes, the seven most dangerous magical books ever written. Luckily, Archie had managed to thwart Barzak's plans to unleash the dark magic, and he had imprisoned the warlock inside the book.

That was only a few weeks ago, and Archie still felt a tingle of fear when he thought about it. It had been a very close call. It had also been very exciting!

"I can't wait to start learning spells," Archie said, turning to Bramble.

"Just one of the many benefits of being an apprentice at Mothballs," she replied.

"Mothballs" was the apprentices' nickname for the museum—because it smelled of old parchment and mothballs. They used the nickname to keep it a secret from the Unready—people who didn't know about magic. Only those who were descended from magical families knew that magic existed.

Archie and Bramble were on their way to the museum now. They were eager to find out what they would be learning this term.

"Just think," said Archie as they left the high street and walked down a secluded cobbled street. "As long as

Thistle passes his Flame test, he'll begin his apprentice-ship, too."

Thistle Foxe was Archie's other cousin, and tomorrow was his twelfth birthday, which meant he would be tested by the Flame of Pharos.

"I know. I can't believe my little brother is all grown up," Bramble replied.

Archie's apprenticeship was at a magical bookshop, the Aisle of White, attached to the museum. Archie and Bramble could see the bookshop in front of them as they turned into a courtyard. A small, insignificant-looking building with a green front door, it had a sign above it in flaking white and gold paint that read: THE AISLE OF WHITE: PURVEYOR OF RARE BOOKS. PROPRIETOR: GEOFFREY SCREECH.

The bookshop served as a place to sort the magic books (unbeknownst to their owners) from other books that people came to sell. It was the only part of the museum that was open to the Unready.

Archie said good-bye to Bramble in front of the bookshop. She worked in the main museum, which was on the other side of the courtyard and strictly off-limits to the nonmagical world. Apprentices went through a secret entrance in Quill's Coffee & Chocolate House.

Archie opened the door to the bookshop and a bell clanged noisily. The Aisle of White was bigger than it appeared on the outside. Dark wooden bookcases stood in columns dividing the shop into a series of aisles. The shelves were full of old books, but the magical ones were kept behind a velvet curtain at the back, waiting to be mended or sent to the museum for classification.

The shop was lit by flickering candlelight. It smelled musty—of candle wax, cobwebs, and old paper.

Geoffrey Screech, the owner, was standing behind the counter writing in a ledger in his neat handwriting. A slight man, with thinning gray hair and a goatee beard, Screech wore a green waistcoat and a yellow bow tie. It was his job to check if any books that came into the shop were magical.

"Morning, Archie," Screech said, glancing up.

Inside an open cardboard box on the counter was a book. "New arrival?" Archie asked.

"Came in yesterday," said Screech. "One of the Unready clearing out the attic. He had no idea it was magical, of course. Anyway, it needs to go down to Old Zeb."

Archie peered at the slim volume. It had a patterned cover with panes of diamonds in red, green, and black. Tied around it was a piece of thick twine.

Archie caught a glimpse of Screech's assistant, Marjorie Gudge, in one of the aisles, putting books on the bookshelves. A short woman with thick glasses, Marjorie was in charge of the nonmagical books.

Picking up the cardboard box, Archie hurried through the black velvet curtain at the back of the shop toward Old Zeb's mending workshop. He glanced at a bookcase behind the curtain as he passed. It was full of repaired magical books waiting to go to the museum.

"Morning, Archie," said a papery voice.

"Hello," Archie replied, glancing at an old book of potions on the shelf. "And how are you today?"

"Much better now that the rip in my cover is mended," said the book appreciatively.

A chorus of other papery voices chimed in, wishing Archie a good morning and inquiring after his health.

Archie smiled to himself. This had become a daily routine. The books talked to him because he was the only one who could hear them.

"Good morning to you all," he said. "Sorry, I can't stop to chat today. I've got to get down to the Mending Workshop."

As Archie moved on down the corridor, he heard a rustling sound from inside the box he was carrying.

"So you can talk to books?" said the curious magical book, who'd never encountered a book whisperer before. "Where are you taking me?"

"To Old Zeb, the bookbinder," said Archie.

"Someone tied me shut with this horrible piece of twine," complained the voice. "It's too tight. I can't breathe. Take it off, would you?"

Some magical books couldn't be trusted. He'd been tricked before.

"We'll see what Old Zeb says," he said.

The book was quiet as he walked along the passage-way, which ended in a spiral staircase leading downward.

Archie took a lantern from a shelf, and, balancing it on top of his box, he began to descend. At the bottom of the stairs he stepped into a long, dark corridor, lit by flaming torches. The air smelled damp and earthy.

Three arched doors led off the corridor. Each was a different color: the first was green, and the second was blue. Archie walked past these. The Mending Workshop was behind the third door, the red one. Beyond it, the passageway disappeared into shadows, and on several occasions Archie had thought he could see a fourth, black door, but it was too dark to be certain.

He knew better than to go exploring down here. His

curiosity had landed him in trouble before. Once he had heard strange noises coming from behind the second door and had sneaked a peek behind it, only to discover a fierce magical creature—a stone griffin called a Bookend Beast—guarding the entrance.

Archie pushed the red door open and stepped inside. The Mending Workshop was a large room with a workbench down the middle and the Word Smithy set into one wall. All sorts of bookbinding tools were scattered along the bench and hanging on racks.

Old Zeb was standing by the Word Smithy, the Flame of Pharos burning brightly inside the little furnace. He was a tiny old man, no more than four feet tall, with white hair that stood up in tufts, a hooked nose, and dazzling green eyes. In the brief time Archie had known the old bookbinder, he'd grown very fond of him.

Damaged books were piled up on the workbench waiting for the old man to repair them, and it was Archie's job to assist the bookbinder and then take the books to the museum for cataloging.

"Ah, mornin', Archie," Old Zeb wheezed. "And what have you got there?"

"New arrival," replied Archie. "Looks like a broken clasp."

"Good lad. Well, pop it on the end of the bench," said Old Zeb, his eyes sparkling. "We'll get to it later. Now I expect you want to hear your report and find out what you'll be learning next?"

Archie nodded.

"Thought so," said the old man, "but first things first. Marjorie has made us a cake to celebrate the start of the new term." He smiled, indicating a large fruitcake in a round tin. "Stick the kettle on, there's a good boy."

Old Zeb never did anything without a cup of tea first. Archie filled up the copper kettle and put it on top of the Word Smithy. As he did, he felt his palm prickling again. The itching was getting worse. It had never bothered him this much even when his Firemark had first appeared.

"Mmmm, you can't beat Marjorie's fruitcake," said Old Zeb a little while later as he swallowed a mouthful and washed it down with a slurp of tea.

He handed Archie a scroll. "Your report," he said. "Go ahead and open it!"

Archie unrolled the parchment and began to read.

Archie is a likeable and enthusiastic boy. He is a talented bookbinder with a real flair for the subject, which should serve him well in the magical realm. His timekeeping could be better, but he makes a lovely cup of tea. Overall, a great start—well done, Archie!

Old Zeb beamed at him. "You're a natural—just like your dad!"

Archie felt a surge of pride. Old Zeb had taught his father when he was an apprentice at the museum. Archie had never really known his parents. His mother and father, and his elder sister, had disappeared when he was still a baby. His gran, Granny Greene, had told him they had been lost at sea when a ferry had sunk in the English Channel.

Old Zeb was speaking again in his high, scratchy voice. "So far, you've learned about the different types of magical books. You won't forget about Poppers in a hurry, eh?" He gave Archie an amused look.

Poppers were magical books with spells that popped out when they were opened. When he had first started, Archie had opened a Popper and released the spell for a knight called Sir Bodwin the Bold, even though Old Zeb had warned him not to touch anything without supervision. Fortunately, the bookbinder had seen the funny side of the situation. Archie smiled at the memory.

Old Zeb continued. "For this term I've prepared some harder lessons for you. You'll be learning more about the three types of magic."

Each of the three branches of magic had its own department in the museum. Natural Magic came from nature—magical creatures and plants; and the sun, the stars, and the seas. Mortal Magic was man-made magic and included magical instruments called astroscopes. The third type of magic was Supernatural Magic, which used the power of spirits and other supernatural beings.

"And you'll be doing some spelling!" Old Zeb said.

Archie couldn't stop himself from grinning. This was what he'd been hoping for. He'd be learning real magic!

"We'll also be looking at tricks and traps that the unwary apprentice can fall into."

The bookbinder rubbed his hands together. "Now, talking of tricks and traps, this is an interesting one," he said, picking up the book Archie had just brought down from the shop. "Unless I'm very much mistaken, it's a Grabber! The bigger ones can be downright dangerous, but even a little one like this can be troublesome."

Archie regarded the book with interest.

"Go on, have a closer look," said the old man. "But

be careful. The twine is to stop it springing open. Grabbers are responsible for a lot of the things that go missing
in Unready households. They're particularly fond of socks
and keys."

The twine was tied very tightly and knotted several
times.

Old Zeb scratched his head thoughtfully. "I think the
best thing is for you to hold it closed while I put a new
clasp on it."

The old bookbinder waited until Archie was in position. "Ready?" Archie nodded.

"One. Two. Three. Go!" Archie leaned his full weight
on the book while the old bookbinder cut through the
twine with a knife and slid it clear.

"Very good." He smiled. "Now don't move."

Archie felt a bit silly using all his strength to keep a
book shut, but Old Zeb usually knew best. He had been
mending magical books for years. How many years,
Archie couldn't begin to guess. It could be hundreds for
all he knew!

Old Zeb took what looked like a large magnifying glass
and held it up to his eye. It was an Imagining Glass, a magical instrument that magnifies the user's imagination—very
useful for seeing something from a different angle, or

getting a new perspective on a problem.

The bookbinder smiled. "You're right, the clasp is broken. Soon fix that."

Archie felt pleased with himself. He was becoming increasingly confident about his book-mending skills.

"Now where is that clasp?" said the old man. "I knew it would come in handy." He rummaged through a battered old tool bag and triumphantly held up a clasp with a silver key.

"There," he said, his quick hands replacing the old clasp with the new one. He held the key between his fingers. "Just need to turn—"

But at that moment something gave Archie a sharp shove from underneath. It was so unexpected that it knocked him off balance. There was a peal of laughter as the book's cover flipped open and a small figure sprang out.

No bigger than a doll, it was dressed in a bright diamond-patterned harlequin costume like a clown and wore a black mask. In the blink of an eye it darted across the bench and grabbed what was left of the fruitcake.

"Hey!" cried Archie, diving toward the cake tin. "Leave that alone."

But it was too late. Before Archie or Old Zeb could

do anything, the figure had melted back into the pages, clutching the half-eaten cake.

Old Zeb clicked the clasp shut and turned the key. The pealing laughter stopped abruptly, and the book vanished in a puff of smoke.

The old man shook his head. "Locking the book after the fruitcake has bolted, I'm afraid," he said ruefully. "That's the trouble with Grabbers. They're so quick.

"Magicians use them for stealing from each other," he explained. "Oh well, it could have been worse. It could have taken my Imagining Glass. I can always ask Marjorie to make us another cake."

Archie smiled. "I suppose that's what you call grabbing a bite to eat!" he said.

Old Zeb's face cracked into a broad smile. They both chuckled.

Archie felt his palm itching again and scratched it. The tickling sensation was definitely getting worse.

Old Zeb gave him a knowing look. "Bothering you, is it?"

Archie nodded.

"Show me." The old bookbinder inspected Archie's hand, where the needle-and-thread symbol was. "You'll be getting your second Firemark any day now."

"But I've still got so much to learn about bookbinding," said Archie, surprised.

"Perhaps you have, but the Flame has other plans for you," said Old Zeb.

The old man slipped on a thick leather glove and opened the door to the Word Smithy. His eyes shone in the firelight.

"It contains the spirits of the ancient Magisters—the old magic writers. When they died, they were cremated in the Flame. The last Magister brought the Flame to Oxford. As long as it continues to burn, magic will never die."

Archie stared at the tongues of fire, writhing in their timeless and ever-changing dance. Suddenly, the flame changed color, blazing with a silver light.

"Good heavens," muttered Old Zeb, a startled look on his face. "It's never done that before."

At that same moment, fifty miles away at the London offices of Folly & Catchpole, the oldest and most secretive law firm in England, Horace Catchpole sat on one side of a highly polished walnut desk. On the other side was Prudence Folly—Horace's boss—and right now she was watching him as a falcon might watch a rabbit.

"And this is it, is it?" asked Prudence, gazing at a gold ring inside a small box on the desk. "This is the second instruction for Archie Greene?"

Horace nodded. "It's all here in the ledger," he confirmed, indicating a large book balanced on his lap.

In the cellars under Folly & Catchpole's offices just off Fleet Street there were hundred of packages containing secrets. Each had its own entry in the client ledger, explaining precisely when and where it was to be delivered.

"I see," said Prudence, raising an eyebrow. "And what exactly does it say?"

Horace opened the book and ran his finger down the page until he found the entry. The grandfather clock in the corner of the room ticked impatiently.

"Well?" demanded Prudence.

Horace peered at the spidery writing through his horn-rimmed spectacles. The writing was faded, but he could make out some of what it said. "One gold ring for Archie Greene, care of the Museum of Magical Miscellany."

Prudence picked up the ring and inspected it. It was made from a gold band shaped like a dragon that curled around to swallow its own tail.

Her brow furrowed in thought. "When you told me there was a second instruction, I thought it would be another magical book like the first one."

She pursed her lips. "And you're sure there isn't anything else that goes with it? Something we might have *missed*?"

Horace shifted uncomfortably in his chair. The last time there had been a package for Archie Greene, he had forgotten a scroll that should have been delivered at the same time. In the end, everything had turned out all right, but Prudence had no intention of repeating the error.

Folly & Catchpole had been the law firm of choice for the magical community of Britain for more than nine hundred years. Its reputation was built on two guiding principles: minding its own business and not making mistakes. Prudence was determined to make sure it stayed that way.

"Just the ring," said Horace, consulting the ledger again.

"Do we know who the client is this time?" asked Prudence.

"There are some initials," said Horace, squinting at the page. "The first letter looks like an *F*, but the second letter isn't clear. The ink is smudged."

Prudence tutted. "Sloppy bookkeeping," she said. "When is it due?"

"When the Firemarks start to appear," said Horace. "And there's an unusual method for delivering it. . . ."

CHAPTER 2

The Strange Firemark

The next morning Archie woke with a start. Someone was shaking him. It took him a moment to realize where he was. His cousin's freckled face peered down at him, and he remembered he was in the bedroom that he and Thistle shared at the Foxes' house at number 32 Houndstooth Road.

"Rise and shine, Arch," Thistle said. "It's my birthday, and I don't intend to miss a second of it. You're only twelve once, you know!"

Archie yawned and stretched. "Happy birthday!" he said.

They dressed and hurried downstairs. Loretta Foxe,

Archie's aunt, was icing a large birthday cake on the kitchen table. She was famous in the Foxe household for her unusual combinations of food. Archie's birthday cake had been chocolate and marshmallow—with sardine filling. This one smelled fishy, too.

Loretta's turquoise eyes lit up when she saw them.

"Happy birthday!" she cried, giving Thistle a hug.

Thistle rolled his eyes for Archie's benefit. But Archie could tell that he was secretly pleased.

"I'm making omelets," Loretta said. "What do you want in them, marmalade or jam?"

Thistle smiled. "I think I'd like to try cheese today."

Loretta raised her eyebrows. *"Cheese?"* she said, making a face. "In an *omelet?* Are you sure?"

Thistle nodded. "Yep, as it's my birthday, I'm going to try something new."

"And you, Archie?" Loretta asked.

"Yes, why not?" Archie said, delighted at the prospect. "I'll have cheese as well."

Loretta looked mildly disappointed.

"Here you go," she said a couple of minutes later, handing a plate to her son. "A *cheese* omelet. And here's a *cheese* omelet for you, too, Archie."

At last, Archie was going to eat something normal at

the Foxes' house. His mouth watered at the thought. He had just picked up his fork when Loretta whispered in his ear.

"Don't worry, I put some jam in to take away the taste of the cheese!" She winked at him, and he felt obliged to wink back, but he felt his appetite disappearing. On a shelf above the stove, a row of cookery books gathered dust. Loretta preferred to cook by instinct.

Just then, Woodbine Foxe ambled into the kitchen. Archie's uncle was a thin man with a clump of straw-like hair that made him look like a scarecrow. He had bags under his eyes, and the lines in his face looked even deeper than usual. Woodbine worked as a finder, tasked with locating magical books that were unknown to the museum. He spent most of his time scouring secondhand bookshops and following up leads.

Occasionally, the museum would send him abroad to track down a missing book. Sometimes he would bring back presents for the children from his foreign travels. He had spent the last week in the Czech Republic.

"What ho!" he called cheerfully, sitting down at the table. "Happy birthday, young'un!"

"Thanks, Dad," said Thistle between mouthfuls of omelet. "When did you get back?"

"First thing this morning," said Woodbine. "I wanted to be here for your birthday."

"How was Prague?" asked Archie.

"A disaster," Woodbine replied. "We had reports of a book in a part of the old city they call Alchemists' Alley. An anonymous tip-off. Gideon Hawke sent me to a bookshop to collect it. But someone else beat me to it."

"Greaders?" asked Loretta, her brow darkening.

Woodbine nodded. Greaders were the sworn enemies of the Flame Keepers. They were called Greaders because they were greedy for magical books and would go to any lengths to acquire them.

Woodbine continued. "They tortured an old man and woman for information about where the book was. That's the second attack this month."

"I thought the Greader attacks were meant to stop once Arthur Ripley was locked up," said Loretta. Arthur Ripley had been behind the Greader plot with Barzak that Archie had foiled. Ripley was now locked away in an asylum for the magically ill.

"That's what we all thought," muttered Woodbine, shaking his head. "But someone else is pulling the strings. And they're very good at covering their tracks."

Greaders usually operated in secret. It was rare for

them to reveal their identities. In public, many appeared to be upstanding members of the magical community. But behind closed doors they practiced dark magic.

Woodbine's eyes narrowed. "Before he died, the old man whispered a name—Amos Roach."

"Well, let's talk about something more pleasant," said Loretta, forcing a smile. "After all, it's not every day that a Foxe turns twelve!"

"Happy birthday, Thistle," said Bramble, sitting down at the table.

———

"Right," said Loretta, when they had cleared away the breakfast things. "There's just time to open some presents before your Flame test."

Thistle's first stop would be the bookshop to receive his Firemark.

"Which mark are you hoping for?" asked Archie.

"Dad started with his Finding mark, so that would be good," said Thistle thoughfully. "But there's all three in the family. Mum was a Minder, and Uncle Alex was a Binder like you. So to be honest, I don't care. I just want to get the Flame test over with!"

Loretta disappeared into the walk-in larder and returned with three presents.

"This one's from Granny Greene," she said. Granny

Greene had raised Archie from a baby, and in all that time she had never mentioned his cousins or the museum. Archie had subsequently discovered that his father had made her promise to keep him away from magic for as long as possible. It was only when a mysterious book had arrived on his twelfth birthday that he had discovered the truth about his magical heritage. It had been Gran's idea that Archie should go and live with the Foxes in Oxford.

Unbeknownst to Archie, she had written his cousins letters and always sent them birthday and Christmas presents. Since Archie had come to live with them, the letters had become more regular. Gran herself was now away on a mysterious journey, and had been traveling for several months.

Thistle opened a white envelope taped to the parcel.

Dear Thistle,

    Happy birthday!

    I wish I could be there to see you off on your first day at the museum. I'm sure you will be a great success and make us all very proud. Here is something that will help you find your way.

                Love,

                Granny Greene

P.S. Say hello to Archie and Bramble for me.

Thistle ripped open the parcel to reveal an old book. *"Magical Places to Visit,"* he said, reading the title. "Brilliant!"

"It was your grandfather's," said Loretta, a trace of wistfulness in her voice. "I recognize it. Dad loved exploring. I'm sure that's where you get it from, Thistle."

"It's got a name written inside," said Thistle. "Gadabout Greene?"

"That was your grandfather's nickname," said Loretta, smiling.

On the back of the book there was a three-sided symbol that looked like a knot inside a circle.

A message was printed beside it in clear black letters.

THIS BOOK HAS BEEN CERTIFIED AS SAFE TO OPEN BY ORDER OF THE MUSEUM OF MAGICAL MISCELLANY, OXFORD, ENGLAND.

All newly discovered magical books had to be handed in at the museum to be inspected for damage. Then they were classified as level one, two, or three in magical power. The more dangerous ones—level three—had to stay in the museum. But levels one and two went back into circulation within the magical realm.

Thistle riffled through the pages. "There's an entry for Quill's," he said. "'Quill's Coffee and Chocolate House was founded in London in 1657 by Jacob Quill. In

1667, Quill moved to Oxford after the original shop was destroyed in the Great Fire of London. Quill's has been in Oxford ever since.'"

"Here's a little something from your father and me," Loretta said, handing over the second parcel.

Thistle tore it open to find a small box. He opened it and held up a silver ring with an orange gemstone.

"We thought you might like it as your Keep Safe," said Woodbine. "It was my father's, but it's been in the Foxe family for generations."

It was customary for a new apprentice to receive a piece of jewelry with a charm on it to give them some protection from dark magic. Bramble's Keep Safe was a charm bracelet, and Archie's was a magical pendant that had once belonged to the famous magician John Dee.

"Thanks, Dad!" said Thistle, turning the ring over in his hand and admiring it.

"It's got a guarding spell on it," said Woodbine. "The gemstone glows whenever dark magic is near."

"And last but not least," said Loretta, handing him the final parcel, "you'll need this. It's your snook—give it to Geoffrey Screech when you get to the bookshop."

It was a tradition at the museum that all new apprentices brought a magical book on their first day to prove they were from a flamekeeper family.

"It was among some old family papers. I found it when I was looking for the ring. It doesn't have a stamp," said Woodbine. "So tell Geoffrey to handle it carefully."

"You'll have to wait for your present from us," said Archie. "Bramble and I want to get you something at the book fayre."

The International Magical Book Fayre was held every five years, and this year it was being held in Oxford at Quill's. The apprentices had been talking about it for weeks. The fayre attracted members of the magical community from all over England and beyond, including magicians and fortune-tellers, and there would be all sorts of magical gifts and other items for sale.

"I can't believe it's this weekend," said Thistle.

"And I can't believe you're starting your apprenticeship today! You're getting so big and grown-up," said Loretta, wiping the corner of her eye. "Now," she said, forcing a smile, "there's just time for some cake before you go!"

⟶

The three cousins walked the half-hour journey into Oxford. As they approached the Aisle of White, Thistle slowed down, dragging his feet.

Archie glanced at Thistle. He wondered what was going through his cousin's mind.

"All right, Thistle?" he asked, punching him lightly on the arm.

Thistle swallowed and gave a nervous smile. "Of course," he said unconvincingly. "Never better. I've been looking forward to this moment all my life."

Working in the Mending Workshop, Archie had seen several apprentices on their first day. Most of them were a bit apprehensive before their Flame test. For all his bravado, Archie could see that Thistle was no different.

He opened the door to the shop. Geoffrey Screech was standing behind the counter as usual, his small round spectacles perched precariously on the end of his long, thin nose. He was wearing his best green bow tie, a sure sign that a new apprentice was expected. At the sound of the bell, Screech looked up and regarded the three children over his spectacles. He gave a friendly smile, showing small teeth.

"Morning, Archie. Bramble. And . . . Thistle, isn't it?"

Thistle swallowed hard and nodded.

Screech opened a thick ledger on the counter and ran his finger down the entries.

"Ah yes, here we are. Thistle Foxe." He glanced up. "Everything seems to be in order."

Bramble pushed her brother forward. "Go on," she said. "He won't bite." She gave Thistle's shoulder a gentle squeeze. "There's a start-of-term meeting in Quill's later. We can all go together. I'll meet you outside. Good luck!"

Bramble opened the door and let herself out of the shop.

Thistle handed Screech his snook. "My dad said to tell you it doesn't have a stamp," he mumbled.

"Very good," said Screech, taking the book. "Looks like an old plotting book. You don't see those very often. I'll make sure it is examined and properly classified. Now, let's get you downstairs to Old Zeb."

Thistle swallowed nervously. Screech called out over his shoulder. "Marjorie!"

His assistant bustled through the velvet curtain.

"There you are, Marjorie. Can you keep an eye on the shop while I take the new apprentice down to the Mending Workshop?"

Screech was in charge of recording the results of the Flame test. He had been keeping the records in his impeccable copperplate handwriting for thirty years.

"Yes, of course, Mr. Screech," said Marjorie. She gave Thistle a smile. "Good luck!"

Archie led Thistle and Screech through the velvet curtain and along the corridor. He took a lantern from the shelf and descended to the corridor below.

⁓

"Thistle Foxe!" said Old Zeb when they reached the Mending Workshop. "I remember you when you were just a baby. Loretta used to bring you into the shop. You never sat still for a moment. Always off exploring something or other. How is Loretta, by the way?"

Before Thistle could reply, the old man's face turned serious. "We heard about that business with Woodbine in Prague. Very nasty," he said. "Apparently they couldn't even identify the victims."

He tutted loudly and shook his head. "What's the world coming to when a bookshop's not safe? Good thing we've got some extra security here," he muttered.

Archie guessed he was referring to the Bookend Beast behind the second door. He wondered again what was behind the green one and whether he had really seen a black door in the shadows at the end of the corridor.

Screech gave a shallow cough to change the subject. "Yes, well, we're not here to talk about what happened in Prague. We're here for Thistle's Flame test," he reminded Old Zeb.

"Yes, yes. Quite so," said the old bookbinder, taking the hint. "Let's see what the Flame has in store for you."

The old man opened the door to the furnace. The fire hissed, releasing a cloud of thick white smoke.

Archie was relieved to see that the Flame appeared to be back to normal after its strange behavior the day before.

Old Zeb's expression turned serious. "Thistle Foxe, do you have what it takes to be an apprentice at the Museum of Magical Miscellany?" he said. "The Flame of Pharos knows," he added mysteriously. "It's been burning for thousands of years."

Archie had heard this speech before several times, and even though he knew what was coming next, the speed of it still caught him by surprise. The old man suddenly pulled a yellow flame from the furnace and hurled it across the room toward a pile of books.

Archie's instinct was to catch the flame, but he managed to restrain himself. It wasn't his Flame test, after all. Thistle shot out a hand and caught the fireball. It burned and flared in his palm, twisting and writhing. Then it changed from yellow to blue and disappeared.

"Show me your hand," demanded Old Zeb. "Ah," he said, inspecting Thistle's palm, where a small blue symbol of an eye had appeared. "The Finding Firemark."

Thistle's eyes gleamed. He looked relieved and exhilarated at the same time. Training to be a finder involved learning how to identify magical books and spot the telltale signs that they might be dangerous. Being a full-time finder like Woodbine was a precarious way to make a living, but it was exciting. It took sharp eyes and a keen nose for magic.

Old Zeb smiled. "There," he said kindly. "All done." He dabbed some balm onto Thistle's hand. "This'll soothe the itching."

He turned back to the Word Smithy and was about to close the door when something unexpected happened.

The flame spat out a spark like a tiny shooting star. It arced across the workshop and then burst into a shower of fiery gold and vanished. Archie felt an intense itching in his palm and stared at a gold mark that had just appeared there.

"Good heavens," cried Old Zeb, gawking first at the flame and then at Archie. "What is it?"

Archie held out his palm so the others could see. Where the Finding, Binding, or Minding Firemark usually appeared, there was a golden mark—it looked like a dragon swallowing its own tail.

Archie was sure he'd seen it somewhere before, but he couldn't remember where. Old Zeb grabbed his hand and ran his thumb over the new mark. Archie watched the old man's face turn a shade of pale that he had never seen before, especially from someone who spent his day working in front of the oldest furnace in the world.

Old Zeb glanced over at Screech. "Geoffrey, I think you should take a look at this."

Screech hesitantly walked over to where Archie and Old Zeb were standing. Archie stuck his hand out for Screech to see.

Screech gasped. "The Golden Circle . . . it can't be! This is the alchemists' mark. The last time it appeared was more than three hundred years ago. Fabian Grey . . ."

He brought his hand to his mouth and looked suddenly anxious. Archie wondered if Screech thought he'd said too much.

"The Alchemists' Club," breathed Old Zeb.

At that moment, the flame shot out a second spark, which flew across the workshop like the first one and exploded with a golden light. There was a cry from Thistle. He was staring at his hand. "Look! I've got another Firemark!"

Sure enough, beside the symbol of the eye, a second Firemark had appeared just like the one on Archie's hand.

"Two alchemists' Firemarks!" exclaimed Screech. "Nothing for three hundred years and then two appear together. . . ."

Old Zeb's brow darkened. "We must inform the museum elders, Geoffrey. They might know what it means. It seems most unusual to me. . . ."

Archie and Thistle left the bookshop with their heads in a spin. After the appearance of the strange Firemarks, Archie had shown Thistle around the Mending Workshop, but they were both very distracted by the appearance of the Golden Circle Firemarks. What exactly did they mean?

Neither Geoffrey Screech nor Old Zeb was able—or was it willing?—to shed any more light on the matter, but they'd promised to call an urgent meeting of the elders. In the meantime, Screech had asked the boys not to discuss the strange Firemarks with the other apprentices.

"Best if we keep it among ourselves," he'd said. "Just for now."

Archie couldn't help thinking that Screech and the old bookbinder knew more than they were saying.

When they left the bookshop half an hour later, Bramble was waiting for them in the courtyard.

"How did you get on?" she asked. "You passed the test okay?" She kept her voice low so that passersby wouldn't hear their conversation.

"Yes, but—"

"Thank goodness for that. We'd never live it down if a Foxe failed the Flame test. Several of the Ripleys and the Nightshade family have failed it over the years, of course. Most have gone on to become Greaders. But the last person to fail was four years ago. So, come on, spill the beans. Which apprenticeship are you starting with?"

"It's a bit more complicated than that," said Archie, casting a glance at Thistle.

"Show me your Firemark," demanded Bramble.

Thistle turned away. But as he did, Bramble snatched his hand and looked at his palm.

"What the hell is that?" she exclaimed when she saw the Golden Circle. "It looks like a snake!"

"It's the alchemists' Firemark," said Thistle sheepishly. "Archie's got one, too. But we're not allowed to talk about it. Old Zeb and Geoffrey Screech said we should keep it to ourselves until the elders have discussed it."

"That doesn't include me, though," said Bramble. "So you'd better tell me exactly what happened, over a hot chocolate."

The three cousins made their way across the small, enclosed courtyard and down the stone steps that led to Quill's, a scruffy medieval building with exposed timbers. They stepped through the front door and were greeted by the delicious smell of chocolate suffused with vanilla, orange, and other mouthwatering flavors.

The interior of the shop was bathed in a warm light. It came from a sunbeam so bright that it was dazzling. This was deliberate, so that people entering the shop wouldn't see the secret entrance to the museum. The shaft of light was called the Door Ray, and it allowed the Flame Keepers to come and go without arousing suspicion.

At the front, Quill's looked like an ordinary café, but at the back there was a much larger space called the back of house. Separating the two parts was a magical wall called a Permission Wall, which was enchanted so that the back of house was invisible to the Unready.

Standing behind the bar was a tall, slim woman with bare arms and lots of tattoos. Both of her eyebrows were pierced. Her name was Pink, and she was the waitress at Quill's. She also controlled the Door Ray by operating a brass lever disguised as a hot chocolate tap. The lever had three positions. In the upright position, the Door Ray was open to everyone. In the horizontal position, it would allow only people with a Firemark through. And in the downward position, the entrance was locked.

Ordinarily, the lever was set to allow only those with Firemarks access to the back of house, but at her discretion Pink could move it to allow visitors in.

Pink could move between the two sides at will, passing along the bar, which ran right through the Permission Wall. Whenever she moved from the front of house to the back of house, her hair changed color from black to pink.

"All right, Bramble?" Pink said when she saw them arrive. "All right, Arch? First day, Thistle? I s'pose you've got your Firemark?"

Thistle nodded self-consciously and kept his hand firmly closed. The Door Ray would automatically detect his Firemark, so he didn't need to show it.

"See you on the other side," said Pink, smiling.

Thistle gazed at the bright beam of light. It would be only his second time in the back of house at Quill's. The first time, Pink had been persuaded to let him through without a Firemark because he was under the protection of a museum elder. This would be the first time he would be entering in his own right.

As the three cousins passed through the Door Ray, they caught the scent of amora—the smell of magic. It always made Archie feel slightly light-headed. Different types of magic had different scents. Natural Magic smelled of nature. Mortal Magic was man-made magic; it smelled of musty rooms and fire smoke. Supernatural Magic smelled otherworldly, of cold tombs and dead flesh—it was Archie's least favorite type of amora. The Door Ray used Natural Magic, and today it smelled of freshly cut grass.

The back of house was full of the most comfortable furniture imaginable. There were squishy leather sofas and chairs that were perfect for flopping into. It being the first day of the new term, the place was buzzing with apprentices. The air was filled with excited chatter about reports and new timetables.

At a table, Archie recognized a sharp-featured woman with silver hair. This was Feodora Graves, the head of the

Supernatural Magic Department.

The three cousins joined the line to get a drink. When it was their turn, Bramble ordered three hot chocolates and led Archie and Thistle to a quiet table in a corner of the room.

"So what's the story with the alchemists' Firemark?" she asked, dropping her voice.

Archie hesitated before answering. He and Thistle had promised not to discuss what had happened with the other apprentices, but he didn't include Bramble in that. She was family, after all.

"Screech said it was called the Golden Circle Firemark," replied Archie in a hushed tone, glancing around to make sure none of the other apprentices was listening. Again, he wondered why Old Zeb and the bookstore owner were being so secretive. "He mentioned something called the Alchemists' Club. And a name: Fabian Grey."

Bramble almost spat out her hot chocolate. "Fabian Grey!" she spluttered. "He's only the most notorious apprentice in the history of the museum! What's he got to do with it?"

"I'm not sure," said Archie. "But Screech was definitely worried about something. That's why he told us to keep it quiet."

"Talk of the devil," muttered Thistle. "Here's Screech now."

The owner of the bookshop had just stepped through the Door Ray and was scanning the room, looking for someone. When he spotted Graves, he went over and spoke in her ear.

"He'll be telling her about the Firemarks," said Archie.

Graves looked up sharply. She glanced across to where the three cousins were sitting.

"She doesn't look very happy," said Archie. Screech said something and Graves shook her head. They both looked over at the cousins again. Screech turned and left.

Graves looked thoughtful. Then she rose to her feet and clapped her hands for silence.

"The meeting is about to start," said Bramble. The elders often took advantage of the fact that all the apprentices could be found in Quill's after work and called meetings if they needed to.

"Welcome back," said Graves in a clear voice. "A new term is upon us, so if you'd like to take your seats, we have some important notices to give you."

Archie, Bramble, and Thistle followed the crowd into the function room at the back of Quill's and sat down. Several of the elders were there already, seated on the raised platform at the front of the room.

Archie recognized a short man in a tweed jacket as Dr. Motley Brown, the head of Natural Magic. Beside him was Gideon Hawke, the head of Lost Books. It was Hawke's job to track down dangerous magical books and make sure they didn't fall into the hands of Greaders. At first sight, he looked very ordinary, but like Archie's, Hawke's eyes were different colors: one was blue, and the other was gray. Hawke was known to be the most magically gifted of the museum elders. He had once saved Archie's life by rescuing him from *The Book of Yore*.

Next to Hawke was Wolfus Bone, a gaunt-looking man with prominent canine teeth. Bone was a magic diviner who worked with Hawke in Lost Books.

On the other side were two people Archie had never seen before: a man with a bald head that resembled a boiled egg and a girl with long auburn hair, who looked a couple of years older than Bramble.

The apprentices were seated now. Graves took her place beside Hawke and Brown and exchanged words with them. Hawke suddenly sat bolt upright, a look of concern on his face. He glanced in the direction of the three cousins.

Graves rose to her feet and clapped her hands again. Her pale green eyes scanned the upturned faces in the room.

"Before we start, I'd like to welcome a new apprentice. Thistle Foxe joins us today."

Heads turned and eyes sought out the newcomer. There was a murmur of interest. Thistle smiled awkwardly. Hawke's eyes bored into him.

Graves continued. "I would also like to take this opportunity to welcome two special guests. Professor Orpheus Gloom is from the Royal Society of Magic in London," she said, indicating the bald man. "He is here to oversee the book fayre."

The Royal Society of Magic was the organization responsible for controlling magic in Britain. It reported to the Magical League, the international magical body. Gloom beamed a smile around the room. His eyes seemed to linger on Archie, making him feel uncomfortable. Did he know Archie was a book whisperer?

Graves was speaking again. "Our other guest is Katerina Krone, from the Prague Academy of Magic. Katerina has won a scholarship to the museum to further her studies. Her research on writing magic was chosen from hundreds of entries from magic students around the world. She has been granted special access to the archives to advance her work."

The girl inclined her head slightly. She had full lips and piercing blue eyes. "I have dreamed of being at the famous Museum of Magical Miscellany," she said, with a trace of an accent. "I am looking forward to exploring the archives to see what light they can shed on the secrets of writing magic."

Graves's lips twitched into what was the slightest of smiles. "Now, as you all know, we are very proud to be hosting the International Magical Book Fayre here at Quill's this Saturday. This is a great honor, and I hope you will all attend."

She scanned the room. "I'm sure I don't have to remind you of the importance of secrecy. We don't want to arouse the suspicions of the people of Oxford. If they thought for one second that there was any magic occurring in the city, it could jeopardize the work of the museum. I am sure I can rely on your discretion.

"Last, but by no means least, I want to talk to you about security. When it was first suggested that the book fayre be held in Oxford, the elders agreed that we would allow members of the magical community not affiliated with the museum onto these premises.

"For the duration of the fayre, the Door Ray will be open to allow those without Firemarks to enter. We must remain on our guard. In recent weeks, there has been a sharp increase in reported Greader activity." She paused. "There was another attack this week—in Prague."

There were concerned murmurs from the apprentices. Graves held up her hand for silence.

"Be assured that although the Door Ray will not be functioning in its normal way, there will be alternative security measures in place. Please be vigilant at all times."

"Now, enjoy the fayre, everyone!"

Archie was making his way out of the function room when he felt a hand on his arm. He turned to see Graves looking at him intently.

"Archie, a quick word," she said. "You too, Thistle."

She steered the two boys to one side.

"It's come to my attention that you have received a very unusual Firemark. May I see?"

Before Archie could reply, she took his hand firmly in hers and examined it.

"Geoffrey's right," she said. "It's the Golden Circle. And you have one, too, Thistle?"

Thistle nodded.

Graves looked pensive. "Well, there's nothing we can do about it now. But report to me first thing Monday. Until then, please keep this to yourselves. We don't want to alarm the other apprentices."

—————

Both boys were thoughtful on the way home. The strange Firemark was weighing on their minds. As soon as Archie got back to 32 Houndstooth Road, he went straight upstairs to their bedroom and took out an old shoe box that he kept under the bed. In it were some of his father's old things that Loretta had kept for him, including some magical reference books.

Archie sifted through the box until he found a book called *Magical Greats: The Good, the Bad, & the Ugly*. It was a catalogue of all the most famous and infamous magical books and magicians.

He flicked through the book until he found the entry he was looking for.

The Alchemists' Club: a group of seventeenth-century alchemists led by Fabian Grey. Like all magic writers, the members of the Alchemists' Club were marked with the Golden Circle Firemark, which they adopted as their symbol. The

Golden Circle is one of the three requirements for writing new magic, the other two being the ink, made from the magical substance Azoth, and an enchanted quill, made from a feather given freely by a magical creature. Grey and his associates set out to rewrite the master spells in the great books of magic. But their magical experiments started the Great Fire of London and led to the introduction of the Lores of Magical Restraint.

Underneath was the Golden Circle symbol that was on Archie's hand.

He read the entry again.

At his old school he'd been taught that the Great Fire of London had started at a bakery in Pudding Lane. But he knew now that this was the Unready version of history, which left out anything to do with magic.

He examined the mark on his hand again. Something was gnawing away at the back of his mind. He had definitely seen the symbol somewhere before. If only he could remember where!

CHAPTER 3

The Magical Book Fayre

A rchie's hand was itching the next morning, but he was determined not to let it spoil his enjoyment of the book fayre.

As they walked into the city center, Loretta was explaining that magical fayres had been commonplace in England right up until the seventeenth century.

"So now the International Magical Book Fayre is the only one in the world," concluded Loretta. "All the others were banned by the 1666 Lores of Magical Restraint."

"It's ridiculous banning the fayres!" growled Woodbine as they passed the Aisle of White and crossed the courtyard toward Quill's. "It just drives the trade in

49

magical books underground. It's almost as daft as banning the use of magic outside of magical premises. How are we supposed to defend ourselves from Greader attacks if we can't use the magic that's in the books?

"Those poor people in Prague," he added, shaking his head. "We don't even know who they were. They were sitting ducks. It's disgraceful. The Magical League should be ashamed of itself."

Loretta shot Woodbine an anxious glance. "Now, now, Woodbine, that's quite enough rabble-rousing from you. Keep your voice down. The Lore is the Lore, whether we agree with it or not," she added in a hushed tone.

Archie had never heard his uncle and aunt talk like this before. He had assumed they were both staunch supporters of the Lores and the magical authorities that enforced them. But he was beginning to realize there were different points of view within the magical realm.

As they joined the line waiting to get into Quill's, Archie was still thinking about what Woodbine had said. It seemed to him that his uncle was right. How could they defend the museum against a Greader attack if they were forbidden to use magic? The Greaders took no notice of the lores. They used magic if they thought they could get away with it.

He remembered his own close shave with the greader Barzak. He had encountered the warlock inside the museum, where magic was sanctioned, and had been able to use his book-whispering talents to defeat him. But what if they had met outside the museum? What would have happened then?

It was a chilling thought. If Woodbine had arrived in Prague in time to save the two people who had been murdered, would his uncle have followed the letter of the Lore, or would he have used magic to defend himself? Archie had another thought: Did book whispering count as doing magic? He supposed it had to, even though he had no control over it.

Perhaps it was time to start trusting people with magic again. Maybe the Golden Circle Firemarks were a sign that the time to lift the lores was approaching?

He was still pondering this when they reached Quill's. A blackboard propped up against the wall said PRIVATE FUNCTION. CLOSED TO THE PUBLIC. This meant that the only people coming in and out of Quill's would be from the magical realm. At least they wouldn't have to worry about the Unready blundering into the fayre by mistake.

A man with a clipboard was standing just inside the front door to Quill's. Tall with a stoop and a permanent scowl on his face, his name was Dr. Aurelius Rusp, and he was one of Archie's least favorite people.

Archie wasn't alone in disliking him. The other apprentices tried to avoid Rusp if they could. Ever since he'd discovered a fire in the museum twelve years earlier, Rusp had become a real grouch. Sometimes, though, he helped out Gideon Hawke in Lost Books. On one occasion this had included spying on Archie.

Pink was standing by the Door Ray.

"Hello, Pink," said Bramble. "How's it going?"

"Fine. But I wish *he'd* lighten up," she said, flicking her eyes to where Rusp was glowering at everyone who entered the café.

Bramble raised her eyebrows. "Why's he here?"

"Extra security," said Pink. "Just for the fayre. The Royal Society of Magic insisted on it."

Rusp watched them intently, his fingers drumming impatiently on his clipboard.

Loretta went to go through the Door Ray, but Rusp put out an arm to stop her. "Name?" he demanded.

Loretta looked at him in disbelief. "Really, Aurelius, I've known you for thirty years!"

"It's my job to keep a record of everyone who goes in and out," Rusp growled. "Name?" he demanded again.

Loretta gave him a black look that she had perfected over many years of parenting.

"Loretta Foxe," she snapped. "And this is my husband, Woodbine, my son and daughter, Thistle and Bramble, and my nephew, Archie—all of whom you know perfectly well!"

Rusp wrote down their names. "Can't be too careful," he muttered darkly. "There could be Greaders about."

Loretta gave Pink an exasperated look.

Pink looked embarrassed. "Go ahead, Loretta," she said.

With a toss of her head, Loretta stepped through the Door Ray, followed by the other three Foxes.

Archie was about to follow when he spotted Arabella Ripley entering Quill's. Arabella had started her apprenticeship at the same time as him and was the granddaughter of Arthur Ripley, the infamous Greader.

Archie and Arabella had got off to a bad start, but she had tried to help him when he was in trouble and had saved the life of the museum's magical diviner, Wolfus Bone, from a dark-magic attack.

Arabella was with her mother, Veronica Ripley, and as usual she looked bored. Peter Quiggley, another apprentice who had started at the same time as Archie, was also there with his parents. Two very tall women, one with red hair and the other with black hair, had entered just behind them.

The woman with black hair was carrying a white stick with an ornate handle.

"Is there a queue, sister?" she asked. "What's causing the holdup?"

"It's a man taking names," said the redheaded woman.

"A man, sister?" said the first woman. "Why ever is he doing that?"

"Security, sister. He says there might be Greaders."

"It's a disgrace!" Archie recognized Veronica Ripley's voice. Veronica was always complaining about something. "Respectable members of the magical community being harrassed like this. I won't stand for it."

"Hurry up, Archie," said Pink.

Archie stepped through the Door Ray, squinting as the light dazzled him. He caught the scent of roses. The next thing he knew, he was on the other side.

He gasped in wonder at the scene that met his eyes. The back of house looked completely different. The function room was three times its normal size and looked like a cross between a medieval fayre, a circus, and a yard sale. Flags fluttered and music played, giving the place a carnival feel.

Archie wondered who among the elders was able to perform such an impressive enchantment. There were tents of all sorts of sizes, shapes, and colors. In among the tents were brightly painted stalls. Straight ahead was a larger tent like a big top.

Woodbine appeared at his shoulder. "What do you think, then, young'un?"

"Amazing!" Archie breathed.

Woodbine's eyes gleamed. "The Fayre is one of the main events in the magical calendar," he said.

"I had no idea there were so many people in the magical realm," said Archie, looking at all the people. "They're not all Flame Keepers, are they?"

Woodbine shook his head. "No, but they all come from magical families. Some were apprentices at the museum and their children are, too, but others attended one of the academies of magic and probably send their children to the same place. Most of them do ordinary Unready jobs when they leave.

"The lucky ones work in magic. They might be freelancers like me, or become elders at the museum. Or, if they're especially ambitious and well connected, they might work for one of the magical authorities—the Royal

Society of Magic or the Magical League. And whether they work in magic or not, they all love to come to the fayre."

He pointed at a flyer pinned to a notice board. In addition to buying and selling books, the fayre also had a whole day of events. Archie, Bramble, Thistle, and Loretta gathered around, and Woodbine read out who was appearing.

"Tent Number Two—at noon today—Martha Stitch, 'Why Bookbinding Needn't Be a Bind.'"

"That sounds interesting," said Archie.

Woodbine continued. "Tent Number One at two p.m.—'Green Magic Is Clean Magic,' a talk by Rusty Gardner, author of *Growing Green Fingers*.

"And then at four p.m. there's a talk called 'Tracing Your Magical Ancestors: Why It's Better to Be Historical Than Hysterical,' by Orpheus Gloom and Katerina Krone."

"Katerina Krone is the student I told you about," Bramble said.

Woodbine scratched his head. "The Krones, they're one of the old Flame-Keeping families like us."

He continued reading the flyer. The main attraction was happening in the big top at five p.m.—a talk entitled

"Why a Magical Creature Isn't Just for Halloween," by Maurice Dancer.

"Oh yes," said Bramble. "Rupert mentioned this—he's going to be helping."

Rupert Trevallen, one of the older apprentices, worked in the Mythical Menagerie in the Natural Magic Department. A tall, dark-haired boy, with chiseled features and a cheerful disposition, he was popular with the female apprentices. Archie suspected that Bramble was among those who had a crush on him, although she would never admit to it.

Loretta took the children to one side. "Now you three stick together," she said. "Here's some money for lunch."

She lowered her voice. "Don't buy any books without a stamp. And don't show anyone those Firemarks. You heard Rusp—there could be Greaders about. And after what happened in Prague . . ." She covered her mouth with her hand. "Well, I don't like to think about it."

Archie, Bramble, and Thistle were having a wonderful time. The fayre was full of fascinating sights, including fire-eaters, stilt walkers, and fortune-tellers using crystal balls and other scrying instruments to tell the future.

Archie spotted a sign above one stall that said, THE

SIREN SISTERS. WE SCRY HARDER!

"I've heard of them," Bramble said. "Hemlock and Delphinium. They call themselves the Siren Sisters, but that's not their real name. They work as a team. Apparently, one is a fortune-smeller and the other is a fortune-yeller."

"Ha! Ha!" roared Archie. "Very funny!"

"No, I'm serious," said Bramble. "Hemlock is blind but can tell your fortune by your scent, and Delphinium shouts out what's going to happen."

Archie gave his cousin a sideways look. "Half the time I can't tell whether you are making this stuff up," he said.

"No, it's all true," said Bramble with a grin.

"I'll tell you what else is true," Thistle interjected. "I'm starving! It's been hours since we had breakfast. The Siren Sisters can wait."

Some of the tents were selling food and drink. One prominent banner offered MOTHER MAREK'S MUSICAL MUFFINS—CHOCOLATE THERAPY FOR ALL AGES. But Archie's favorite was a slogan for a fizzy drink: DRINK POP UNTIL YOU POP! it said. ORIGINAL RECIPE WITH REAL TUPPENNY RICE AND TREACLE. LOW PRICES. WEASELS WELCOME!

They bought two chocolate muffins each and sat down to eat them. The muffins played a different tune every time they took a bite. With their tummies full, they moved on to explore the other tents.

Most of them were selling old books. The sign that caught Archie's eye was MAGICAL MYSTERY TOURS. Underneath, it explained: ALL THE INFORMATION THAT A MAGICAL TOURIST COULD WANT.

"That's right up Thistle's street," Bramble said. "Where is he?"

"He said he was going for another of Mother Marek's muffins," said Archie, looking at a dusty book. "Can't say I blame him," he added, smiling to reveal chocolate-colored teeth.

"Well, Mum said to stay together," said Bramble, "especially now that you two have got the Golden Circle Firemarks. He should know better than to wander off."

"Let's look in there," said Archie, pointing at a sign that said AGATHA'S EMPORIUM OF MAGICAL MEMORABILIA. ARTIFACTS AND ASTROSCOPES. "Thistle loves astroscopes. We might be able to find him a birthday present."

Astroscopes were magical instruments, which included crystal balls, Imagining Glasses, and other magical devices. Archie had seen some at the museum.

They ducked inside the tent. There was no sign of Thistle, but there were lots of interesting astroscopes to look at. In front of them was a glass cabinet lined with a thick piece of black velvet. Various strange-looking objects had been carefully laid out.

There was a selection of crystal balls of various sizes. Some were clear and others had a milky appearance like very large pearls or looked to be full of smoke. There were other curious objects, too, including some that resembled pocket watches in silver and bronze cases, a silver-topped walking stick, and a selection of mirrors—some of them silver like normal mirrors and others made of black glass. There were also shallow silver scrying bowls used by fortune-tellers.

The stallholder, Agatha, was a short, birdlike woman with lank black hair and large gray eyes. She was wearing a green smock and had a brightly colored shawl wrapped around her shoulders.

"Hello, my dears. What can I do for you? Interested in a gift for a friend or family member?"

"We're looking for a birthday present for my cousin," said Archie. "He's just started his apprenticeship at the museum."

"I've got a nice lucky charm at a reasonable price.

The previous owner died suddenly, but don't let that put you off."

"Erm, it doesn't sound very lucky . . . ," mumbled Archie.

"Or how about a nice crystal ball?" suggested Agatha.

"We were thinking of something a bit more . . . exciting," said Archie. "He likes exploring. Have you got anything like that?"

"I've got the very thing," declared Agatha, "a curiosity compass." She opened the glass cabinet behind her and took out a brass instrument that looked like a pocket watch. She flicked open the lid to reveal a compass with a design of a sun on its face and a black needle.

"The needle spins when it detects high concentrations of magic," explained Agatha. "Very popular with explorers for finding magical places—dragon hoards and that sort of thing."

"It's perfect!" exclaimed Archie. "We'll take it."

Agatha put the compass in a wooden box, wrapped it with blue tissue paper, and handed it to Archie. She was watching him intently.

"What's that around your neck?" she said.

Archie put his hand to his chest. His shirt had come unbuttoned so that the Emerald Eye, his magical pendant, was visible on its silver chain, and the stallholder was staring at it.

"That's John Dee's scrying crystal!" she said. "I've seen pictures of it. I'm right, aren't I? Dee was the greatest scryer England had seen in centuries. Some of his scrying instruments are in the British Museum." She shook her head. "Wasted there, of course! But the Emerald Eye, that's a bit special, that is."

Her sharp little eyes regarded him suspiciously. "How did you come by it?"

"It was a present," Archie mumbled. John Dee's ghost had warned him when he gave him the pendant that it was powerful—so powerful that others desired it. Greaders found it irresistible.

The way Agatha was peering at the green gemstone was making him nervous. Was she a Greader?

"You don't see many pieces of that quality," she said, licking her lips. "How much do you want for it?"

"It's not for sale," said Archie.

"Well, can I just hold it for a moment?" asked Agatha, reaching out a clawlike hand with long, dark fingernails. Now she was really worrying him.

"No," he said, taking a step back and quickly rebuttoning his shirt. Agatha's beady eyes followed his movements.

He thought he saw her hand twitch.

"Please yourself," she said. "But if you change your mind, you can find me at my shop in Oxford market. Just ask for Agatha!"

So she wasn't a Greader after all. If she had been, she would have tried to take the pendant. Feeling relieved, Archie and Bramble moved away.

———

"There he is," cried Archie, a little while later, spotting Thistle.

"About time!" groaned Bramble. "We've been looking all over."

"We got you a present," said Archie.

"Happy birthday, little brother," said Bramble, handing him the neatly wrapped gift.

Thistle tore open the tissue paper and opened the box. "It's brilliant!" he said when they explained what it was. "I can't wait to try it out. Look, the needle's spinning."

"It must be all the magic at the fayre," said Archie.

The three cousins strolled into the big top. The first person they saw was Old Zeb. He was in conversation with Orpheus Gloom. When he saw Archie, the old man beckoned him over.

"We were just talking about you," he said. "Orpheus

has a special interest in magical talents."

"Wonderful to meet you at last, Archie," said Gloom, shaking his hand warmly. "It's not every day that I meet a book whisperer!"

Archie smiled awkwardly. So Gloom knew about his unusual ability. Archie wondered what else he knew.

"The Royal Society of Magic is very interested to learn more about the nature of magical talent," continued Gloom. "We know it runs in families, for example. And your case is particularly interesting. . . ."

"Yes, well, don't alarm the boy," said Old Zeb. "Have you tried the musical muffins, Orpheus?" he added, changing the subject. "They're very good. I had one earlier that played the Hokey Cokey!"

The children moved on.

"What did Gloom mean by that?" Archie asked.

"Do you think Old Zeb told him about the Fire-marks?" said Thistle.

Archie hesitated. "No, he told us to keep it a secret. But I suppose the elders might have told him."

Thistle stopped by the WE SCRY HARDER sign they'd seen earlier.

"I've still got some money left," said Thistle. "Let's give the Siren Sisters a try."

He darted past the sign and into the interior of the tent. Archie and Bramble trailed after him. Archie wasn't at all sure he wanted his future read, especially after receiving the alchemists' Firemark. The ghost of John Dee had told him it was dangerous to look too far into the future.

"I'm not sure about this," he mumbled to Bramble as they ducked under the canvas awning.

"I know what you mean," agreed Bramble. "Fortune-tellers are a bit odd. Especially these two!"

They could see the two women who had been behind them in Quill's sitting inside the tent. Archie now noticed just how odd they were. They were of indeterminate age, somewhere between thirty and sixty—it was hard to be any more precise. The first one had jade-green eyes and flaming red hair that spilled down her back like volcanic lava. She wore a long green cloak, with knee-length brown boots.

The other woman had glossy black hair and wore a black leather coat. She was staring blankly straight ahead. He could see now that she was blind. In one hand she held her white stick and with the other clasped her sister's arm. Around her wrist she wore a bracelet with a wolf on it.

Despite their differences, there was a family

resemblance. The two women were talking to Katerina Krone.

"We've traced our family tree all the way back to the Great Library of Alexandria and beyond," the redhead was explaining. "The Nightshades are a very old magical family."

"How fascinating," said Katerina.

"And what about you, my dear?" said the dark-haired sister, sniffing. "Krone is one of the old family names, too."

"Actually, I'm adopted," said Katerina. "My parents died when I was very young."

"How terrible for you. Do you know your original family?"

Katerina opened her mouth to speak, but the redhead, Delphinium, cut her off.

"Later," she said, her eyes flashing. "We have other visitors. A brother and sister, and their cousin. They want to know what the future holds for them."

Hemlock smiled. "Very well."

"We've got money," Thistle blurted out, holding out a coin.

"Excellent," purred the redhead, taking the coin from his hand and dropping it onto a silver tray. "I am

Delphinium. It's a pleasure to meet you. Thistle Foxe—you should be wary of your curiosity. It will lead you into trouble."

Hemlock sniffed deeply. "And you, Bramble, must remember that you are stronger when you stand together than when you stand apart."

Her nose twitched a second time and she pulled a face that suggested she'd caught a whiff of something unpleasant.

At that same moment, Delphinium's head sagged forward like she was in a swoon.

"What is this? Who are you?" Hemlock cried, turning toward Archie.

"I'm Archie," he replied falteringly. "Archie Greene."

"I cannot read you. Your future is hidden from me. Two paths are set before you, but which will you take?"

Delphinium's head suddenly jerked back and she began to yell, "THE BOY HAS THE FORKS ON HIM! ARCHIE GREENE HAS THE FORKS ON HIM!"

Archie stared at her. He felt queasy. His mouth had gone dry and his stomach felt like the bottom had dropped out of it. Delphinium's shouts were so loud, he was sure everyone at the fayre could hear.

"Quick," cried Bramble, "let's get out of here."

She grabbed Archie and Thistle, and they fled from the tent, pushing past Katerina, who was standing at the entrance and had overheard the conversation. Delphinium was still yelling after Archie. It sounded like something about a raven and a warning, but Archie didn't catch it all. Outside, a crowd was gathering to see what all the shouting was about. People were pointing as the three children pushed their way through. Archie could hear voices whispering.

"That's him. That boy is the one she means."

Archie could feel his cheeks burning. A clearing had suddenly opened around him as people scattered. A mother scooped up her child and pulled her close.

In Archie's haste, he ran headlong into someone. Aurelius Rusp.

"Watch where you're going!"

"Sorry, Dr. Rusp," Archie apologized. "But I'm in a hurry."

Rusp scowled at him. "I can see that. But it won't do you any good, boy. You can run, but if you've got the forks on you, then you cannot hide."

Rusp saw the confusion on Archie's face. "It means you've got a forked fate," he added.

Archie brooded over what Rusp had said all the way home from the fayre.

He made a mental note to look up forked fate first thing on Monday morning when he got to the workshop.

"You're very quiet, Arch," said Thistle later, when they were settling down to sleep in the bedroom they shared. "Are you worrying about what the Siren Sisters said?"

"You saw how people reacted," said Archie hotly. "They couldn't get away from me fast enough. It's as if they think bad luck is catching!"

Thistle propped up his chin on his hand. "I wouldn't take too much notice of Hemlock and Delphinium," he said. "The Nightshade family has always been a bit weird. They're known for their batty predictions. Some people think they're descended from Hecate—the witch who wrote *The Grim Grimoire*. Load of old nonsense, if you ask me."

The Grim Grimoire was one of the Terrible Tomes, the seven most dangerous magical books ever written. Five of the seven were locked in the crypt inside the museum. *The Grim Grimoire* was one of the two still at large.

Archie didn't feel at all sleepy. His mind was still turning over the events of the last few days. A lot seemed to have happened in a short space of time. He couldn't help feeling it was all connected in some way.

"I wonder what Graves is going to say on Monday about the Firemarks," he said aloud. "Thistle? Thistle?"

But there was no reply. Thistle was already asleep.

CHAPTER 4

The Hole in the Wall

On Monday morning, Archie walked into Oxford early. He and Thistle were to report to the elders at nine and had arranged to meet in Quill's so they could go together. But he wanted to look up a couple of things first.

The bookshop wasn't open yet, so he let himself in with his key. When he got to the Mending Workshop, he went straight to the shelf of reference books. He took down the first book Old Zeb had ever shown him: *A Beginner's Guide to Magic* by Miles Mudberry. In a section called "Curses, Hexes, and Omens," he found what he was looking for.

FORKED FATE: Someone has the forks on them if their destiny hangs in the balance. The outcome is determined by a decision they have to make. A number of those with forked fates turned to dark magic, including the dark warlock Barzak and Hecate the witch.

No wonder people were nervous when they heard he had the forks on him! They must wonder if he was going to become a Greader!

He took another reference book from the shelf, *Magic Collectors Past & Present*, and looked under *H*.

HECATE was a darchemist, a writer of dark magic, who wrote a book of diabolical spells called *The Grim Grimoire*. According to legend, a bolt of lightning killed Hecate as she was trying to complete the final spell, giving rise to its name, the Unfinished Spell.

Archie felt a lump in his throat. But the book didn't say that he *would* become a darchemist, only that he *might*. He wondered what decision he had to make. Did he have to choose between dark and light magic? That was easy—he would choose light! But perhaps it wasn't that simple.

Archie was still digesting this information when he heard Old Zeb come in.

"Doing some research, eh? Good lad, but I thought you were seeing the elders first thing." Archie explained that he was on his way.

The old bookbinder opened the Word Smithy and studied the flame. "Well, it looks all right today," he muttered. But he had barely finished his sentence when a spark shot out of the Word Smithy and burst into a golden cascade. It was followed by two more.

"There it goes again!" cried Old Zeb, shaking his head. "I think the elders need to see this for themselves. Nip upstairs and tell Geoffrey. He'll have to let them know immediately. They can hold the meeting here."

Archie did as he was told and then returned to the workshop. A little while later there was a knock on the door and Old Zeb opened it. "Come in," he said. "Excuse the mess."

Graves, Hawke, and Brown, the three heads of department, filed into the workshop. Wolfus Bone, the magic diviner, was just behind them and had Thistle with him. Bone glanced at the Word Smithy. "Geoffrey said that the flame had been behaving oddly again?"

"Quite right," said the old man. The door to the

ancient furnace was still open. They all peered in. The flame was burning normally.

"Yes, well, it seems to be all right now," said Old Zeb. "But there's the business of the Firemarks."

"Yes," said Graves. "The Firemarks. That's what I wanted to talk to the boys about."

She waved Archie and Thistle toward the stools at the workbench. They sat down and focused their attention on Graves, who remained standing.

"The Golden Circle Firemark has a special meaning," she said, glancing at Hawke before continuing. "It denotes the ability to write magic."

Archie started. No one at the museum had been able to write magic for centuries.

"We've been waiting a very long time for it to appear— three hundred and fifty years, to be precise," she said. "Frankly, we had imagined that when it did, it would be on one of the older and more experienced apprentices."

She paused. "We will do whatever we can to help you, of course, but it won't be easy. To understand why, you need to know a little of its history."

She paused for a moment. "Two major events have shaped the history of magic. The first was the fire at the Great Library of Alexandria in 48 BC. The second event was the Great Fire of London in 1666, which was caused by a group of young magicians calling themselves the Alchemists' Club."

Archie was desperate to know more.

"Their names were Braxton Foxe, Roderick Trevallen, Felicia Nightshade, Angelica Ripley, and Fabian Grey." She paused, weighing her words carefully.

"They were the last apprentices to have the Golden Circle Firemark."

Archie and Thistle were sitting in rapt attention now.

"On the night of September 2, 1666, a baker's shop in Pudding Lane owned by Thomas Farrinor was set alight. The fire raged for three days and burned down half of London. The authorities said that the fire started in the baker's oven. And that is what the Unready believe to this day. But as you all know, that's not what really happened.

"The truth is that the Alchemists' Club used the baker's cellar for their magical experiments. On that ill-fated night, something went badly wrong, causing the inferno. The authorities thought the people of London would be frightened if they knew that magic was responsible, so they blamed the baker.

"The king knew the real cause and insisted that it must never happen again. The Royal Society of Magic was founded, and Lores governing the use of magic were brought in. Those Lores are still with us now."

"And a very good thing, too," said Brown. "Where would we be without them?"

The doorbell clanging in the bookshop upstairs and the sound of running footsteps interrupted him. They heard footsteps on the stairs and the voice of Geoffrey Screech. "You can't go down there!"

"What on earth is that racket about?" Graves cried. The footsteps stopped outside the door, and someone knocked loudly.

Graves opened the door. Standing outside were Arabella, Bramble, and Rupert.

Arabella had a shocked look on her face and was staring at her hand.

"We're in the middle of an important meeting," said Graves. "Whatever is the matter with you, girl?"

"This!" whined Arabella, holding up her hand so that they could all see the Golden Circle on her palm.

"Another one," said Graves. Her face looked pale. She exchanged looks with Hawke and Bone. "That makes three."

"Erm, five actually," declared Bramble, holding up her own palm to reveal a fourth Golden Circle. "Show them, Rupert."

Graves's eyes opened so wide that they looked like they might pop out. "Not you as well?" she gasped, shaking her head, as Rupert opened his hand to reveal another Golden Circle.

Hawke's brow darkened. "So, now we have five alchemists' Firemarks, just like the original Alchemists' Club," he said.

⁓

The elders seemed unsure what to make of this latest development. They told the five children that they would receive additional lessons that the heads of the magical departments would devise. Until then, they were to go about their usual business, remaining especially vigilant. Under no circumstances were they to discuss the Golden Circle marks with any strangers.

⁓

Archie and Bramble had decided to take Thistle on a tour of the museum. A line of apprentices had formed in Quill's.

"It's very slow today," said Bramble. "I wonder what's up."

Ahead of them in the queue, they spotted Rupert.

"What's the holdup?" she asked him.

"There's something wrong with the Door Ray," said Rupert.

Pink was standing behind the bar, pulling on the brass lever that controlled the secret entrance. The lever was in position to let everyone in, and it was refusing to budge. Sweat was running down her face, and she looked flustered. Rusp was scowling next to her.

Fortunately, there were no Unready customers in the café. Pink gave the lever one more tug, but it still wouldn't move. Shaking her head, she gave up and waved the apprentices in. One by one they slipped through the Door Ray.

Archie, Bramble, and Thistle were among the last.

"What's up?" Bramble asked Pink.

"I knew it was a bad idea to open the Door Ray to people without Firemarks," grumbled Pink. "Now it's jammed."

She glanced at the lever.

"And if that wasn't bad enough, there's something wrong with the Permission Wall," she said. "It's been on the blink ever since the fayre. And all at a time when we're supposed to be on high alert for Greader attacks."

First the Firemarks and now the Permission Wall: Archie couldn't help but think that it was all connected in some way. If only he could figure out how. He thought again about his forked fate. What was the decision he had to make?

Archie wondered how safe the museum was. The

Permission Wall was the first line of defense, but he consoled himself that there were other spells protecting the museum from unwanted visitors. Any intruder who found a way through the wall would still have to navigate the Seats of Learning, a set of ancient flying chairs that transported the apprentices from Quill's to the main museum. The seats required a Motion Potion to work and were activated by Pink, using a set of levers disguised as drinks taps.

There were other areas of vulnerability. Archie had discovered another way into the museum, behind the blue door at the Aisle of White. There were rumors of other entrances, too, at secret locations around Oxford known only to the elders.

On the other side of the Door Ray, the three children were greeted by Pink, now with her trademark pink hair. She was making Motion Potions.

"What's it to be?" she asked.

"I'll have a Shot-in-the-Dark," said Bramble. "In a choc-tail," she added, licking her lips. Motion Potions came in lots of different flavors, and the apprentices could choose to drink them with hot chocolate as a choc-tail, or with fruit juices. A Shot-in-the-Dark tasted of wild berries and citrus.

"I'll have the same," said Archie. "Thistle?"

Thistle consulted the menu of Motion Potions pinned up behind the bar. "I think I'll have a Wild in the Woods," he said.

"Coming right up," said Pink. "And which Seat of Learning will you be using?"

"The Box Seats," said Bramble, "unless they are already taken?" Each seat had its own history and served a different magical department. Some, like the Box Seats, allowed more than one apprentice to travel together.

"They'll be back any second," said Pink, lining up three glasses. She took down an old-fashioned bottle from a shelf. She poured two drops of a thick crimson liquid into each glass, adding a few drips from a blue bottle and a drop from a black bottle to two of them, and from a bright green bottle to the other. The first two glasses gave off a thick white vapor and the third a brown fug. Then she tipped the glasses into three tall mugs and topped them up with steaming hot chocolate.

"Two Shots in the Dark," she said, "and a Wild in the Woods for you, Thistle."

They collected their Motion Potions and crossed the room to the nooks where the Seats of Learning were located. Thistle was gazing around him, wide-eyed.

"Wow! What's that?" he asked, pointing at what looked like the claw of a huge creature protruding from the floor. It was about two feet across and covered in waxy black leather like alligator skin. The claw was open so that its palm formed a seat that was big enough for two people.

"That's the Dragon's Claw," said Bramble. "It's one of the oldest Seats of Learning, but no one uses it anymore. It's got a bad reputation."

"Come on," said Archie, ushering Thistle toward a small nook on the other side of the room. "Pink's waving at us; we must be next."

The Box Seats were a row of ancient wooden theater seats behind a red-and-gold curtain. The three cousins buckled themselves into their chairs and closed the curtain.

"Bottoms up!" said Archie, clinking his glass with Thistle's.

They downed their Motion Potions. Archie's fingers and toes had just begun to tingle pleasantly when the floor opened and the Box Seats plunged through the gap.

The next thing they knew, they were hurtling through the underground passages and caverns that led to the Museum of Magical Miscellany.

Bramble swung her long legs and waved her hat every

time they went around a bend, whooping with delight. Archie joined in with her. It didn't matter how many times he rode on the Seats of Learning, they never ceased to amaze him. It was like the best-ever roller coaster ride and flying all rolled into one. Sharing it with his cousins made it even more fun.

He caught sight of Thistle's flushed face and grinned back at him. Just then the tunnel ended abruptly and they flew into the Bookery, a large cavernous space, where magical books flew around like flocks of birds.

All around them flying books swooped and soared, dodging out of their way at the last moment.

A light shone in the gloom ahead. The Box Seats flew toward it, descending in a series of circles and coming to a halt in a long corridor called the Happy Landing.

"We're here," said Archie, unclipping his belt and hopping out of his seat. "Come on. Quick."

"That was brilliant!" cried Thistle, his eyes shining with excitement. "Even better than I expected. Can we do it again?"

"You'll be doing it every day," said Bramble, smiling. "And if you ever get bored with the Box Seats, there are lots of others to try."

"Come on," said Archie, striding along the passageway

toward a tall oak door with a symbol of a flame. He pushed the door open and stepped inside.

"The Museum of Magical Miscellany!" he declared.

"Mothballs!" exclaimed Thistle breathlessly, his eyes growing even bigger. "I can't believe I'm finally starting my apprenticeship."

"This is the Great Gallery," said Archie, indicating the massive high-ceilinged room they were standing in. On each side, oak staircases led up to smaller galleries. The walls were jammed with bookcases crammed with old books.

As usual, the museum was full of apprentices working. Most of those working in the Great Gallery were doing their Minding apprenticeships like Bramble. They made sure all the magical books were in good order and filed in the right place.

The Finders were assigned to one of the three magical departments: Natural, Mortal, or Supernatural Magic. They learned to identify which sort of magic a book contained. There was usually only one apprentice bookbinder at a time, which was Archie at the moment.

The air above their heads was filled with flying books, flapping their covers like wings. Thistle stared at them in awe.

"Incredible!" he gasped.

Archie managed a smile. Bramble had explained to him on his first day that there was an enchantment on the building that allowed some of the books, those with a special stamp, to move. It saved the apprentices work, because the books filed themselves.

⁓

Later, as they sat in Quill's, Archie asked the question he'd been thinking about all day.

"So what happened to the Alchemists' Club after they started the fire?"

"I don't really know," admitted Bramble. "No one talks about it."

"And Grey?"

"Disappeared. That's the real mystery. Probably just as well after what he'd done. And to think that he started his career as an apprentice at the museum—all five of them did!"

Katerina was sitting at the next table with Arabella. She was examining Arabella's hand. Then she checked her own as if she half expected to see that another Golden Circle Firemark had appeared there.

Arabella was complaining as usual. "It's not fair. You should have received the Firemark instead of me," she whined. "I don't even want it!"

"Well, I'm pleased for you," said Katerina. "The important thing is that the Firemarks are back."

"But why me?" moaned Arabella.

"The Flame decides," said Katerina. "You know that. But if there's anything I can do to help, just let me know. I've researched the Alchemists' Club, so I know quite a lot about them."

Perhaps Katerina knew what had happened to Grey, Archie thought. But just then something else caught his eye. An old lady's face was peering at him through a gap in the Permission Wall into the back of house.

"Look at this, Mabel!" the old woman was saying to her friend. "There's a room back here and it's full of teenagers!"

Pink approached the old lady. "Sorry, madam," she said. "But I'm going to have to ask you to sit down."

She gently steered the old lady away from the Permission Wall and back to her table.

Pink placed her hands over the hole. Her lips moved as she uttered a spell.

> *"Enchanted wall, strong and true*
> *With this spell I renew!"*

Strands of silver mist appeared, and the gap in the Permission Wall closed.

The old lady was cleaning her spectacles with her handkerchief.

"These are for you," said Pink, giving her a bunch of blue flowers. They were called forget-me-nows, and they had a magical scent that made people forget what they had just seen.

"Thank you, dear," said the old lady. "How strange. I thought I saw something, but I can't remember what it was now."

Her friend was patting her hand. "Never mind, dear. It must be something in the tea. What pretty flowers. Such a lovely scent. Where did they come from?"

The first old lady stared at the bunch of blue flowers in her hand. "I really don't remember," she said.

Pink had crossed over to the back of house and was talking earnestly with Feodora Graves, their voices low. From where Archie and his cousins were sitting, they could hear the conversation.

Pink was shaking her head. "I don't understand it," she was saying. "It's felt thin ever since the fayre. It's never happened before."

"And it must never happen again," said Graves.

"Something is attacking the museum's defenses," said Gideon Hawke, who had just joined them.

Orpheus Gloom arrived. "What's all this about a

security breach?" he asked, directing his question at Pink.

"It's all under control," Pink replied tersely. "There was a temporary breakdown in the Permission Wall, but it has been repaired now."

"Thank heavens for that," said Gloom. "I'll ask Rusp to help you out for a while."

Pink didn't look pleased about this. She was pointing out where she had repaired the hole. Archie tried to listen in, but they had dropped their voices to a low whisper.

By now word had spread about the problem with the Permission Wall, and a crowd of apprentices had begun to gather.

"I will ask Morag to check *The Book of Charms*," said Hawke, sweeping past the crowd as he left the room.

~

That evening, at the London offices of Folly & Catchpole, Horace Catchpole was working late, checking the client ledger. He was just closing the book when he heard a sound at the window that made him jump.

Tap, tap.

Horace ran his hand through his thinning hair and composed himself. By now he should be used to the odd ways of the firm's more eccentric clients, but they still caught him by surprise sometimes, even when he was expecting them.

He opened the blind and peered out. A large black bird was perched on the outside of the windowsill and stared back at him. It tapped its beak on the glass again.

Tap, tap.

"I wondered when you'd show up," said Horace, opening the window.

The raven hopped inside and regarded him with flinty black eyes.

"You'll be wanting this, I suppose?" said Horace, holding up the gold ring with the dragon design. "It's to be delivered to Archie Greene at the Museum of Magical Miscellany. But you probably know that already."

The raven turned its head to one side and looked at the ring.

"I don't suppose you can tell me exactly when you will be delivering it?" Horace continued. "Just for our records, you understand. It's my boss, you see. She likes things to be in order. Less chance of mistakes that way!"

The raven gave him a beady-eyed stare. Then it snatched the ring in its claw and flew away.

Horace watched it go. "Flippin' ravens," he muttered, closing the window. "Why can't they make an appointment like everyone else?"

CHAPTER 5

The Book of Charms

When Archie arrived at the Mending Workshop the next day, Old Zeb was waiting for him at the door.

"There you are, Archie. No time to lose. Urgent job. Gideon Hawke has asked us to take a look at a very special book. He specifically asked for you. Come along."

The old man marched back down the corridor where he had just come from. But to Archie's surprise, instead of going back upstairs to the bookshop, the old bookbinder stopped outside the green arched door.

"It's a shortcut," he explained, seeing the question on Archie's face. "Ordinarily, I'd only use it in an emergency, but the Door Ray at Quill's still isn't fixed, so it'll be easier."

Archie watched, fascinated, as the old man took a silver key from his pocket and fitted it into the lock. Then he addressed the door:

> *"Door of mystery, door of grace,*
> *Take me to my chosen place."*

He gave three knocks on the door and added, "Lost Books Department, please."

Then he turned the key and opened the door.

"Come along, Archie," he called as he stepped over the threshold. "Don't dawdle."

Archie followed the old bookbinder through the door and to his amazement found himself standing outside Gideon Hawke's office.

"But . . . how . . . what . . . where?" he mumbled, turning to look for the door he had just come through, only to find that it had vanished. All that remained was a keyhole in the wall.

"Good, isn't it?" said Old Zeb. "It's called an enchanted entrance," he explained. "It can take you to any magical place, as long as you've got the key."

"It's amazing," said Archie, still gazing at where the door had just been. So now he knew what was behind the green door.

Old Zeb's eyes twinkled. "I try not to use it too often, because I need the exercise," he said, patting his stomach. "But while the Permission Wall is acting up, you can use it. I keep the key with the others. Just remember to lock it afterward."

"I thought I saw another door at the other end of the passageway?" said Archie.

The old man frowned. "There used to be a door there once," he said, "but it was sealed more than three hundred years ago. There was an accident and an apprentice died. Now come on—we mustn't keep Gideon waiting."

Hawke was seated behind his desk, with Morag Pandrama and Wolfus Bone gathered around him. All three were focused on a book on the desk. It was a thick volume with a red-and-gold cover and spine. Hawke was examining it through his silvered Imagining Glass.

"Zeb. Archie. Thank you for coming." He put the Imagining Glass down on the desk. "I've asked you here to get your opinion about this," he said, pointing to the book.

Old Zeb peered at it. *"The Book of Charms,"* he said. "Well, I never!"

He turned to Archie. *"The Book of Charms* contains the master spells that protect the museum. The last

Magister wrote it when he founded the museum."

"Yes," said Hawke. "I asked Morag to retrieve it from the secret vault where it's kept. Take a closer look, Zeb." He offered the old bookbinder his Imagining Glass.

The old man took it and studied the pages.

"Oh dear," he declared, shaking his head. "Oh dear, oh dear." He made a tutting sound, sucking through his teeth. "This is dreadful."

The writing in the book was so faint it was barely legible. It looked like it had been bleached in the sun.

Hawke met Zeb's eye. "The charms are fading," he said. "And as they do, the magic protecting the museum fades with them. Once the master spells are erased completely, their magic will be, too."

"The Permission Wall?" said Archie.

Hawke nodded. "Yes, it is losing its power. And soon the spells will be so faint that it will fail completely. And it won't stop there. The spells guarding the Terrible Tomes will also be affected. And there is the Darchive to consider."

"Oh my," said Old Zeb. "We wouldn't want the charm on the Darchive to fail." Archie's ears pricked up. What was the Darchive? "How long has this been going on?" Old Zeb asked.

"We don't know," said Hawke. "Pink noticed the Permission Wall was wearing thin after the fayre. Have you ever seen anything like it before?"

Old Zeb was staring at the open pages of the book. "No," he said, shaking his head. "In all my time as a bookbinder, I've never come across anything quite like this."

"What about you, Archie?" asked Hawke. "Can you try to speak to the book? Maybe it can tell us what ails it."

"I can try," Archie said, desperate to help if he could. He closed his eyes and concentrated on *The Book of Charms*. He reached out in the silence with his mind, trying to connect to it. Nothing.

He opened his eyes and glanced across at the book, willing it to speak, but it remained silent. He shook his head. "No, I'm sorry, it's not responding."

Wolfus Bone held a forked twig lightly between his fingertips and approached the book. This was the magical divining rod he used to test for magical strength. The rod twitched once and then was still.

"I'm not surprised," said Bone. "The book is very weak. The magic is running out. Nothing lasts forever."

"Yes, I suppose you are right," said Old Zeb. "We can only mend and make do for so long. Eventually, all the books will fade."

"But why is *The Book of Charms* fading so quickly?" said Hawke. "Something is draining its power. Is there anything you can do to slow it down, Zeb?"

The old man shook his head. "Nothing that I can think of," he said forlornly. "I'm used to repairing books, but this is beyond my knowledge. If only it was something simple, like a torn cover or some loose leaves. This requires a magic writer. No one else can help the book."

As they made their way back to the Mending Workshop, the old bookbinder was not his usual chirpy self. Archie could tell that he was shaken by what he'd just seen.

Old Zeb had said that only a magic writer could help *The Book of Charms*. The master spells had to be rewritten—and quickly. It was the only way. And only someone with the Golden Circle Firemark could write magic.

Archie felt a sudden thrill. This was it! This was what he had to do. He had to persuade the other four apprentices to help him write magic for the first time in three hundred and fifty years. He felt light-headed as he thought about the enormity of the task.

But even as the idea crystallized in his mind, he realized there was no way Hawke would agree to it. Not after what had happened before. The Alchemists' Club had tried to write magic and it had gone spectacularly wrong. Now he was contemplating doing the same thing. But this time it would be different. They wouldn't make the same mistakes.

⌒

That afternoon, the five apprentices sat at a table in Quill's. They had been excited about the start of term and the book fayre, but now things had suddenly turned very serious.

"Ever since we got the Firemarks, everyone seems to be watching us," said Rupert quietly. He was right. Several of the other apprentices were casting curious glances in their direction and whispering in low voices. "It's as if we're meant to do something, but we don't know what it is."

Archie thought he did. He explained what he'd found out about *The Book of Charms*. "If the spells keep fading, then the magic that protects the museum will fail," he said, glancing around at the other four. He wanted to tell them his idea, but he wasn't sure how they would react. He took a breath.

"If *The Book of Charms* isn't rewritten, then we might as well put a welcome sign on the door. The Greaders can walk in and help themselves to any books they fancy."

"Over my dead body," said Bramble hotly.

"Exactly. Someone's got to stop them," said Archie. "The original Alchemists' Club was formed to rewrite the magical books, right?" They all nodded. He continued. "Now, just as the magic is fading, the Golden Circle Firemarks suddenly appear again."

"Where are you going with this, Arch?" asked Bramble, her eyes wide.

Archie took a deep breath. "I think the Flame is trying to protect the museum," he said. "That's why it gave us the Firemarks. Not even the elders can write magic. We're the ones with the Firemark, so we're the only ones who can do it."

The other four looked at him. It took a moment to sink in.

"But we haven't got the faintest idea how to write magic," said Arabella.

"I've been thinking about that," said Archie. "Fabian Grey and the others found a way to write magic, so we can. We know the knowledge is somewhere in the museum, because they found it. I think we should re-form the Alchemists' Club," he said.

"But none of us have even finished our apprenticeships," said Arabella.

"That's true," said Archie. "But neither had they, and

they did it. If we all pool our knowledge, we can, too!"

"Well," said Rupert, "I suppose I could show you the menagerie and explain what I know about Natural Magic. That wouldn't be hard."

"Exactly," said Archie.

"What about Hawke and the other elders?" asked Rupert.

Archie shook his head. "It'll have to be our secret," he said. "Hawke thinks we're too young. What do you say? Are you up for it?"

This was the moment of truth. He held his breath. The other four apprentices exchanged glances.

"Archie's right," said Bramble quietly. "The elders can't write magic. They don't have the Golden Circle Firemark. We're the only ones who can do it. We can meet in secret, just the five of us—no one else needs to know."

"So, is that a yes?" asked Archie.

Bramble hesitated for a moment longer and then nodded. "There was a Foxe in the original club, and there will be a Foxe in the re-formed club," she said. "I'm in!"

"Make that two Foxes," said Thistle.

"And a Trevallen," said Rupert. "Arabella?"

Arabella looked away. "Come on," said Archie. "There was a Ripley in the original club, after all."

"That's what worries me," snapped Arabella. "My family doesn't have a good record with this sort of thing. Several of my ancestors were Greaders, and my grandfather tried to kill you!"

"Just because you're a Ripley doesn't mean you have to become a Greader," said Archie.

Arabella paused and took a breath. "It still sounds dangerous to me. Look what happened with the original Alchemists' Club. Do we want to take that chance?"

"If Archie is right, then we don't have a choice," said Bramble. "If we don't rewrite the spells, then no one will, and the museum will be destroyed!"

"But we don't know where to start," said Arabella.

"We don't. But there's someone at the museum who does," said Archie. "Katerina. She's studying how to write magic. If anyone knows what we need, then it's her."

"Well, she did offer to help. I suppose we could ask her," said Arabella.

"Brilliant!" said Bramble. "That's agreed then. The Alchemists' Club rides again! We can hold our first meeting tomorrow at—"

But she never got to finish her sentence, because at that moment a dark shape arrowed through the Door Ray and landed on the table. Arabella screamed.

Bramble's eyes opened wide as she stared at a raven. In its claw it gripped a gold ring.

"What on earth . . . ?" said Bramble.

The raven flapped its wings noisily. There was a sudden hush as people turned to look. For a moment the bird gazed around the room, taking in its surroundings. Its flinty eyes came to rest on Archie. Then, to everyone's surprise, it spoke.

"Archie Greene, I have come from the tower to warn you. The five have been revealed, but there is unfinished business.

"The forks are on you. Choose your path carefully. I bring this ring as a sign that I speak the truth."

The raven dropped the ring on the table. The other apprentices in Quill's crowded around, pointing at it and whispering in low voices. Archie's mind was racing. The Siren Sisters had said something about a raven. But what was the warning? And what was he supposed to do about it?

All these thoughts passed through his mind in a split second as he stared at the ring on the table.

For a moment nobody moved, and then Feodora Graves eased her way to the front. She had been talking to Pink about the Permission Wall.

"Goodness, what a fuss. Haven't you ever seen a raven before?" she demanded.

"Not one that talks," muttered Meredith Merrydance, in a voice that was louder than she intended.

Graves gave her a withering look. "Anyone would think you'd never heard of magic!"

"It's a bad omen," declared Enid Drew.

"Nonsense," said Graves. "It's a talking raven, that's all. They're very clever birds."

Archie's mind was still racing. The raven was watching him, its head cocked to one side.

Graves picked up the ring and examined it.

"What does it mean?" asked Meredith.

Graves was still thinking about her reply when another voice interrupted.

"I would have thought that was perfectly obvious." The apprentices turned their heads to see Aurelius Rusp at the back of the room. Archie hadn't known he was there, but he had witnessed the whole episode. "Archie Greene has the forks on him."

His pronouncement was met by another outbreak of excitable chattering among the apprentices.

"Aurelius!" warned Feodora Graves, holding up the ring between her thumb and forefinger. "It's Fabian

Grey's ring—it bears his mark."

At that moment, the raven snatched the ring from her. It swooped over the table and dropped it into Archie's hand.

"Beware the Alchemists' Curse!" it screeched.

Then it flapped its wings and disappeared through the front door, leaving a stunned silence.

CHAPTER 6

The Dragon's Claw

In Quill's the next morning everyone was talking about the mysterious raven. Many of the apprentices had seen it and had heard Rusp. Those who weren't there at the time had received dramatic accounts from their friends.

"It was amazing," Archie heard Peter Quiggley telling one of the other apprentices, a boy called Gabriel Monk. "The raven said that the museum was cursed."

Archie's ears pricked up.

"And it gave Archie Greene a ring! They say he's got the forks on him, too. And you know what that means? He could be a darchemist!"

Gabriel's eyes opened wide. "Really?"

Archie ignored them and hurried past. If people wanted to talk behind his back, that was up to them. He thought about the ring, which was still in his pocket. Why had the raven given it to him? What was he supposed to do with it?

He found his cousins at the bar. They were excited about the first meeting of the new Alchemists' Club, which was going to take place that lunchtime. As far as they were concerned, the appearance of the raven just made it more urgent.

"I'll have a Black Death," said Thistle, when Pink asked them what Motion Potions they wanted. "And I'll be riding in the Dragon's Claw."

"You're brave," said Pink. "It's pretty wild."

Thistle's eyes gleamed. "I know. I read about it in *Magical Places to Visit*!"

"Well, it's up to you," she said. "The last person who used the Claw ended up in one of the dungeons in the Supernatural Magic Department and was an hour late for his apprenticeship. I'll get to you as soon as I can, but there's a couple of others in front of you."

She moved to the end of the bar to serve someone else.

Bramble gave Thistle a dark look. "With everything else that's going on, do you really think you should be using the Dragon's Claw?"

"Where's your sense of adventure, Bram? I'll be fine," Thistle said dismissively. "Besides," he added, patting *Magical Places to Visit* in his pocket, "it's all explained in here. It sounds really exciting."

Pink handed him a glass with a thick black substance like tar.

"One Black Death," she said.

"That looks disgusting," said Bramble, pulling a face. "Anyway," she added, dropping her voice so that no one could overhear, "we're meeting Rupert and Arabella in the West Gallery at noon. Don't be late!"

"We'll need to find somewhere more private once we start meeting regularly," said Archie.

"You're right—we can't practice writing magic in plain view of the elders," she said. "Try to keep him out of trouble," she added, nodding at Thistle. "He won't pay attention to me."

Bramble collected her Motion Potion and made her way toward the Box Seats.

"Listen to this," said Thistle, reading from his book. "The Dragon's Claw belonged to Fellwind the Destroyer, one of the great dragons of the North. His claw was so large that it could hold two men. It has an unusual spinning motion."

Archie wasn't sure he liked the sound of the Dragon's

Claw. But Thistle had a gleam in his eye, and Archie could see that he wasn't going to change his mind. His adventurous cousin didn't know the museum very well, so Archie decided he'd better go with him. At least that way if the Claw let him off in an unfamiliar place, he could guide him back to where he was meant to be.

"Okay," he said. "If you insist on using the Claw, I'm coming with you."

He ordered another Black Death, and the two of them made their way to the nook called the Den and approached the giant talons. Thistle scrambled up into the seat and made himself comfortable. Archie joined him.

"Now what?" he asked.

Thistle consulted his book again. "'To operate the Dragon's Claw, pull the thumb forward and drink the Motion Potion. . . .'"

"Right, here goes then," said Archie. He pulled the thumb forward. The talons closed around them.

"Bottoms up!" he said, clinking glasses. The Black Death tasted of licorice.

Thistle was gazing at the book in his hand. His expression had changed from anticipation to apprehension. "Uh-oh!"

"What's the matter?" asked Archie.

"I didn't read the next page. There's more! Listen to

this. 'The Dragon's Claw is rarely used because it has a reputation for trickery and treachery.'"

"Well, you were warned, and it's too late to do anything about it now," said Archie, spotting Pink giving them the thumbs-up signal. "We'll be at the Happy Landing in a moment."

The Dragon's Claw began to spin, corkscrewing its way into the floor. As it did, Thistle cried out. Perhaps it was scarier than he had expected. But Archie was soon too frightened for himself to worry about his cousin.

The Dragon's Claw flew along the dark tunnels under Quill's, spinning ever faster. The lights from the lanterns were just a blur as they hurtled through the narrow passages.

Its movements were far more violent and unpredictable than the other Seats of Learning. From time to time they would touch the wall of the tunnel, which sent them ricocheting off it and causing the Claw to lurch to one side or another. The spinning in particular was very disorienting; it meant that Archie couldn't be sure where he was going. He felt giddy.

Finally they shot out of the tunnel and into the Bookery. Archie felt a sense of relief that the wild ride must be nearly over. He wouldn't be in a hurry to use the Dragon's

Claw again. Just then he ducked as an unfortunate book collided with the top of the Claw, making a horrible thudding sound. He heard an indignant yelp from the book, and the air was full of fluttering loose leaves like feathers. Then they were plummeting toward the ground a long way below.

Archie felt sick now. He tried to look at Thistle, but with all the spinning he couldn't turn his head to see the expression on his cousin's face. Then he closed his eyes. They must be nearly at the Happy Landing by now, he thought. Unless the Dragon's Claw was taking them somewhere else?

They had slowed down. The Claw was spinning in place now. Archie glanced across at Thistle, trying to catch his cousin's eye. Thistle's pale face gazed back at him. He looked decidedly green around the gills.

There was a grinding sound as an ancient lock was drawn back, followed by the groan of a heavy door opening. Archie opened his eyes a little, but all he could see was darkness. The Dragon's Claw moved forward again and the door slammed shut behind it.

Archie thought they had stopped spinning, but it was so dark that he couldn't be sure. He couldn't even tell that his eyes were open. He put his hands to his face and touched his eyelids. They were definitely open; he could feel his eyelashes fluttering against his fingertips.

"Thistle, are you all right?" he asked, reaching out and touching his cousin's shoulder.

"Yeah, I think so."

Archie was trying to orient himself. He couldn't even tell which way was up and which way was down. He could be upside down, for all he knew. The only thing he was sure about was that this wasn't the Happy Landing that he'd arrived at so many times before. A shiver traveled up his arm.

Archie pushed the dragon's thumb away and the Claw opened. Still feeling woozy, he slithered out onto the ground.

Archie felt around him and discovered that he was now sitting on what felt like some cold flagstones. He got to his feet. For a moment, he swayed, with his head still spinning. He heard Thistle land beside him. And he thought he heard something else; a rustling sound. It was very faint, but in the darkness his other senses were heightened. He turned his head toward the sound. There it was again.

"Where are we?" Thistle asked, his voice hoarse with fear.

"Beats me," said Archie. "But wherever it is, it's not where we want to be." He swallowed hard. "And I don't think we're alone."

~

The next few hours were the longest Archie could ever remember. At first the boys tried to find a way out. They felt their way back to the entrance. They banged on the heavy door, shouting for help, but no one came.

After a while they slumped down with their backs to the door and sat side by side. In the oppresive darkness, every minute dragged by. They were tired, cold, and hungry, and they were also becoming increasingly frightened. They jumped at the slightest sound. Archie was beginning to think they might be trapped there forever.

"Why did I have to try the Dragon's Claw?" groaned Thistle. "Why didn't you stop me?"

"Bramble and Pink tried to warn you," said Archie. "But you wouldn't listen."

"Well, I'm listening now," Thistle said, sighing.

Archie was thinking about his forked fate again. There was something very wrong, and he was sure it was connected to the Golden Circle Firemarks and *The Book of Charms*—and now this. "I think someone or something brought us here," he said.

"What for?" asked Thistle, his voice shaking slightly.

"I don't know," said Archie. "And I don't think we should wait around to find out. Let's try the door again." He gazed into the darkness. A sound made him start.

"Thistle, did you hear that? It sounded like an animal."

"All I can hear is that rustling sound," said Thistle.

Archie stared blindly into the darkness. He felt a sense of dread like an icy hand on his shoulder. He heard Thistle's voice beside him.

"Archie, I don't want to worry you, but my ring's glowing. Dad said it does that when there's dark magic nearby."

They heard the rustling sound again. The air smelled foul. Just then Archie heard a voice.

"What have we here? Two boys lost in the dark. How delicious!"

Archie blinked into the darkness. "Who are you?" he asked.

"Who are you talking to?" asked Thistle.

"That voice," said Archie. "Can't you hear it?"

"No," said Thistle.

It must be a book then, Archie thought. "Who are you?" he demanded again, edging closer to his cousin.

"Who am I?" the voice taunted. "Who are *you*? That is the question."

Archie could feel his heart pounding. He had goose bumps on his arms, and the hairs on the back of his neck prickled uncomfortably. He did not trust the voice, and he did not trust his own to reply. He felt the palm of his hand itching and opened it to take a look. The Golden Circle Firemark was glowing an angry red.

There was a sharp intake of raspy breath. "So, *you* have the alchemists' mark. How delicious!" exclaimed the voice, and it began to recite a rhyme.

> *"In dark places where none may go*
> *Shadows linger from long ago*
> *Secrets lurk from older days*
> *Hidden paths and stealthy ways*
>
> *Some have tried to find their way*
> *To make the darkness go away*
> *But the choice is yours to make*
> *The fork you take decides your fate"*

Archie tried to memorize the rhyme.

"What is this place?" he demanded.

The voice gave a cracked laugh. "Still don't know, eh? You really are in the dark!"

He heard a sliding sound like something heavy being dragged across the flagstone floor. The stench got stronger. It smelled like something rotting. When the voice spoke again, it was closer.

"I can help you write magic. I can set you upon the right path, book whisperer. I can show you where the others went wrong."

"What others?" Archie demanded.

"The ones who came before you. They had the mark, too, but they made mistakes. "You could be the next great darchemist," said the voice. "Of course, if the elders even suspected it, they'd revoke your apprenticeship! They wouldn't let you stay at the museum!"

"Who are you?" demanded Archie.

Silence.

Archie looked at his hand. The Golden Circle Firemark was still glowing brightly.

———

Morag Pandrama, the museum's archivist, was working late. She was filing away some old scrolls when she thought she heard something. It was very faint, but it sounded like a boy's voice.

It was coming from the far end of the Archive—the section called the Darchive. But no one had been in there for years.

"Help!" it cried. "Get us out of here!"

Pandrama hurried toward the sound. The Darchive was behind a very large door with iron studs and a heavy lock. A grim-faced gargoyle crouched on each side of the door. It was off-limits even to her.

The voice was coming from inside. Pandrama tentatively knocked on the door.

Someone gave a knock in reply, and she almost leaped out of her skin.

"Who's in there?"

After a moment's hesitation, a voice answered.

"Thistle Foxe and Archie Greene. We're trapped in here!"

Morag Pandrama's eyes opened wide. "I'm going to fetch Gideon Hawke," she said. "He'll know what to do."

A few minutes later, Archie and Thistle heard Hawke's voice.

"What on earth are you doing in there?" he demanded.

"We took the Dragon's Claw and something went wrong." Archie's voice sounded thin even to himself.

"But how did they get inside? The Darchive hasn't been opened for years!" said Wolfus Bone.

"Yes," breathed Hawke, "twelve years, to be precise. The last person to go inside was Arthur Ripley, when he was head of Lost Books. Ripley locked it straight afterward, and no one has been back since."

"You can't open it now," said Bone. "Who knows what dark magic dwells within?"

"I don't think I have any choice," muttered Hawke. "It's either that or leave them in there."

There was a long pause. Then Archie and Thistle heard someone take a key chain from his pocket and fiddle with it. A key was fitted into the lock and turned. The door swung open with a loud groaning sound, and the two boys tumbled out before Hawke slammed it shut again.

Wolfus Bone sniffed the stale air that had entered the room with Archie and Thistle.

"What is it, Wolfus?" asked Hawke urgently.

Bone shook his head. "I thought I smelled something," he said thoughtfully.

⁓

It was after midnight when Archie and Thistle arrived back at number 32 Houndstooth Road. But by the lights on in every room, they knew that the other members of the Foxe household were very much awake.

Loretta opened the door to find Gideon Hawke on the doorstep with one hand protectively on Archie's shoulder and the other on Thistle.

"There you are!" she exclaimed when she saw them. "We've been worried sick!"

Thistle gave a sheepish grin. "Good to see you, too, Mum," he said. "And yes, we're all right. Thanks for asking."

Loretta regarded him with wide eyes. "But where have you been?"

Hawke answered. "We found them in the Darchive, Loretta."

Woodbine appeared from the kitchen. "The Darchive!" he growled, and his face looked even more crinkled than usual.

Hawke nodded. "Someone or something bewitched the Dragon's Claw to take them there."

"Do you think it's the . . . old trouble?" asked Woodbine.

"I don't know," said Hawke.

Loretta interrupted. "Well, they've had enough scares for one night. It's time you were in bed," she said to the boys. "Now off you go."

What was the old trouble Woodbine had referred to?

Archie wondered as he and Thistle climbed the stairs. And what was the voice he'd heard in the dark? He wondered whether he should tell Hawke about it. But something the voice had said made him hesitate. His thoughts were interrupted by Bramble, who was on the landing outside her bedroom.

"What happened to you two?" she demanded crossly. "Rupert, Arabella, and I waited for almost an hour."

They'd missed the first Alchemists' Club meeting! Trapped inside the Darchive, they had forgotten all about it. Bramble was fuming, but she calmed down when they explained what had happened.

"Well, I did warn you about the Claw," she said when they'd finished. "But I suppose that's a pretty decent excuse."

"We wouldn't have missed the meeting unless it was something serious," said Archie sheepishly. "Anyway, what did the three of you decide?"

"Nothing really. When we realized you weren't coming, we rescheduled the meeting for tomorrow night. Arabella is meeting Katerina to find out what she can from her."

"There's something else going on," said Archie. "It's to do with the curse. Seems like none of the elders want to talk about it. And when Uncle Woodbine hinted at it just now, your mum shut him up, too."

~

When Bramble and Thistle were tucked into bed, Archie crept downstairs to get a glass of water. He was still thinking about everything that had happened in the last two days. These latest developments were alarming. There had been no mention of a curse until they had re-formed the Alchemists' Club. As he passed the serving hatch to the dining room, he could hear a murmur of voices.

The kitchen was lit by the moonlight coming in from the window. He poured himself a glass of water and took a long drink. He was on his way back to bed when he heard Hawke's voice.

"Now that the five have been revealed, we must find a way to protect them," he said.

Archie paused by the serving hatch. It was open a crack, and he could hear the conversation. He knew he shouldn't eavesdrop, but he couldn't help himself.

"It was such a long time ago," said Loretta. "Surely it couldn't happen again?"

"I fear it might," said Hawke. "This episode with the Dragon's Claw is a worrying development. After what happened the last time, we can't afford to take any chances."

"What will you do?"

"I will investigate," said Hawke. "But the children mustn't write any magic. Not yet. Not until we have some answers. I've called a meeting of the elders for tomorrow evening."

"I hear there was another attack last night," Loretta said. "A woman in Edinburgh, apparently. Killed in her house and the place searched. Is that right?"

"Yes," said Hawke. "A woman called Flora McDuff. These are dangerous times, Loretta. We fear they were after the same book they tried to get in Prague. If it is Grey's notebook, then it's vital that we get it first."

So that was what Woodbine had been sent to Prague for—Fabian Grey's notebook! It must contain some very important information. Archie's uncle had arrived too late in Prague, but the Greaders hadn't managed to get the book either. Perhaps they had suceeded in Edinburgh. Archie's hand itched. He looked down at his palm. His Firemark was burning brightly again.

CHAPTER 7

Two Meetings

I think today would be a good day to start your spelling lessons," said Old Zeb. It was the day after Archie and Thistle had had their scare in the Darchive.

"Never know when this stuff might come in handy," he added with a wink.

The old bookbinder was sitting on a stool at his bench.

"Magic is all around us, Archie," he continued, opening his arms. "Think about it. How else could a sunrise be so beautiful every time, or a flower be so exquisite? This is naturally occurring magic—it is a spell written by creation itself. But magicians need a magic writer to create a spell they can use.

"When the magic of starlight or sunshine is captured in a spell, it is transformed into Mortal Magic. When that first spell is written down, it is the master spell. It binds the magic to the words of the spell.

"I'll show you." The old man held up the needle that he had been using to repair a book. "See this? Because I know a sewing spell from a book of magic, I can simply recite it. Watch.

"Needle sharp, needle true,
Do the work you were made to do."

As Archie watched in amazement, the needle leaped from the old man's hand and began to bob in and out of the spine of the book, making the repair on its own.

"It's the master spell that gives the words their power. Now you try one. Here," said the old man, passing Archie a book. "To start with, you'll need to read it out—just until you know the words well enough to recite it. This is a nice one."

Archie looked at the words on the page.

Kettle hot, and kettle cold,
Do exactly as you're told.

Piles of paper, pots of glue,
Tidy up as you should do.
Rinse the cups and scrub the floor,
Make them tidy as before.

Archie spoke the spell. Nothing happened.

"Concentrate now," said Old Zeb. "No one ever did magic without concentrating."

He tried again. This time the kettle leaped onto the hot plate.

"There, that's better!" chuckled the old man. "Thirsty work, this spelling business. Nice cup of tea is just what we need."

Archie took the hint and took out two chipped mugs from the cupboard.

Old Zeb held up his finger. "Now remember, the master spell binds the magic to the words," he said. "But if that master spell is broken or erased, then the spell loses its power.

"Your Firemark means that one day you will be able to write master spells—but one step at a time. Now it's almost lunchtime, so off you go. Use the enchanted entrance. But remember to put the key back when you're finished."

⏜

That evening the newly re-formed Alchemists' Club was meeting. It was quiet in the museum at night, which was one of the reasons they had rescheduled for that time. Archie and his cousins had told Loretta and Woodbine that they were doing some research. Pink barely raised a pierced eyebrow when she saw Archie, Bramble, and Thistle arrive. It wasn't unusual for apprentices to come in during the evenings to catch up on their work.

The children had agreed to meet in the West Gallery. Off to one side there was an alcove with a leather sofa and a desk and chair for reading. They were pleased that there was no sign of Rusp. It would make it easier to keep their meeting secret without him prowling around.

Rupert and Arabella already knew about Archie and Thistle's misadventure in the Darchive. It had been the main topic of conversation at the museum all day. Archie and Thistle had been receiving some strange looks from the other apprentices. People were all wondering whether it had anything to do with the Alchemists' Curse.

When they were tucked away in the alcove out of sight, Archie placed the gold ring on the table so that they could all see it.

"It's the Golden Circle symbol, all right," said Rupert. "Graves said it belonged to Fabian Grey."

"But why did the raven give it to me?" asked Archie.

"Perhaps it's a Keep Safe," said Arabella, twisting a brooch with a red gemstone in her hand. "I've got this lucky brooch. It used to belong to my grandmother."

Bramble jangled the gold charm bracelet on her wrist. "I'm wearing mine," she said.

"Me too," said Thistle, showing off his ring with the orange gemstone. "Mum thinks we're in danger," he added. "She's in a right old flap about it."

Archie reached inside his shirt and felt the reassuring touch of the Emerald Eye.

"Well, I don't have a Keep Safe anymore," said Rupert. "The lucky cuff links my grandfather gave me were swallowed by Simon the red-bellied salamander last week. I took them off for a moment to clean his pen and he ate them."

"I suppose it might have been worse," said Archie. "You could have been wearing them at the time!"

Rupert smiled. "That's true, but I'd still feel safer if I had one."

"Well, we didn't come to talk about Keep Safes. Let's make a start," said Archie. "I declare the first meeting of the new Alchemists' Club open!" He rubbed his hands together.

"And I have news," said Rupert, holding up a piece of

dog-eared parchment. "This was among some papers that belonged to my ancestor Roderick Trevallen. It's a copy of the oath the original members made when they founded the club. Listen to this:

> *"I swear allegiance to the Alchemists' Club. I promise to do all I can to restore magic to its former glory."*

The five members had signed their full names underneath.

"Every club needs some rules," said Bramble, "and the new Alchemists' Club is no exception. We should take the oath at the start of every meeting. I'll go first.

"I, Bramble Thornbush Foxe, swear allegiance to the Alchemists' Club. I promise to do all I can to restore magic to its former glory."

Bramble grinned. "Your turn, Arabella," she said.

"I, Arabella Ebony Ripley, swear allegiance to the Alchemists' Club. I promise to do all I can to restore magic to its former glory."

They carried on around the circle until it was Archie's turn.

Archie closed his eyes. "I, Archibald Obadiah Greene, swear allegiance to the Alchemists' Club. I promise to do all I can to restore magic to its former glory."

"Obadiah!" exploded Rupert. "Your middle name is Obadiah?"

Archie shrugged. "Yes. Obadiah was the last librarian of Alexandria and my ancestor. What of it . . . ?"

"It's a bit, well, unusual," Bramble said.

"And Thornbush isn't?" snickered Arabella.

"So my parents have a thing about plants," said Bramble with a shrug of her shoulders. "Besides, you're a fine one to talk—Ebony?"

Arabella tossed her head. "Anyway, I have some news, too," she said. "I asked Katerina about the Alchemists' Club, and she told me that they had a secret meeting place. Fabian Grey had a laboratory somewhere inside the museum where he did his magical experiments. And that's where they used to meet."

Archie's ears pricked up. They would need a secret place to meet. "What happened to it?" he asked.

"Katerina thinks it's probably still there, hidden somewhere in the building," said Arabella. "She's trying to find it."

"Shhhh," said Thistle. "There's someone coming!"

They could hear voices approaching. The five children ducked behind a bookcase. They were just in time to see Graves and Brown file past. Orpheus Gloom was with them.

"Thank you for inviting me along," Gloom was saying to Graves. "It's such an exciting moment to be at the museum."

"You are here to represent the Royal Society of Magic," said Graves. "Whatever we decide, the authorities will have to be informed."

"Of course," said Gloom.

"And we would also value your opinion in your capacity as a magical assessor."

Their voices faded as they climbed a marble staircase that led to Lost Books. In their hiding place behind the bookcase, the children exchanged looks.

"Hawke said he was calling a meeting about *The Book of Charms*," whispered Archie. "It must be tonight."

"Don't we need to know what they're talking about to see if we can rewrite the magic?" Bramble asked.

"Yes," said Archie. "And I get the feeling they're not telling us the whole story. Come on."

As stealthily as they could, the five apprentices crept up the first set of stairs leading to the Scriptorium, the unused room set aside for writing magic. Lost Books was on the next floor, up a second staircase. They had just reached the top step when they heard voices coming from

Hawke's study. One of the double doors was slightly ajar.

At first they couldn't hear what was being said, so they crept a little closer.

"Something else has been woken up by the Firemarks," Hawke was saying, "something dark. We must ensure our apprentices don't meet the same fate as Grey and the others."

What did Hawke mean by the same fate as Grey? Was there something besides the Great Fire, something even darker?

"Don't be such an old worrywart, Gideon," said Gloom. "If history teaches us anything, it is that we can get stuck in the past. It is time for magic to move on."

"Besides," he added, "we don't have a choice. Amos Roach is back."

There was more murmuring among the elders.

"Roach?" Brown sounded alarmed.

"It's true," said Graves. "We have been tracking him. He has been seen in Oxford."

"Wasn't he an associate of Arthur Ripley when he was head of Lost Books?" asked Brown.

"Yes, he was linked with the plot to snatch the Terrible Tomes twelve years ago. He disappeared shortly after. There are rumors that he is part of a secret network of Greaders," Graves added. "And we know he was

responsible for that terrible business in Prague and Edinburgh."

"But you know what happened the last time someone
tried writing magic," objected Hawke. "The same thing
could happen again."

"Darchemy?" gasped Graves.

"Yes," said Hawke.

In the passageway outside, the five children exchanged
anxious looks.

Hawke continued. "Barzak had the Golden Circle
when he was an apprentice. So did Hecate and the writers
of the other Terrible Tomes."

Archie's stomach dropped through the floor. He had
just remembered where he'd first seen the Golden Circle
Firemark. It had been on Barzak's clawed hand when the
dark warlock had confronted Archie in the Crypt.

Hawke was still talking. "Until now the threat we
have faced has been a Greader attack on the museum. But
what if a new darchemist emerged, someone who could
write dark magic? Or what if one of the children were to
start writing dark magic, even by accident?"

"I told you it was dangerous," mouthed Arabella.

But Archie wasn't taking any notice of her. He was
too startled by what he'd just heard. The voice in the dark
had said Archie could be the next great darchemist—and

if the elders knew, they'd make him leave the museum. Archie couldn't take that chance.

Gloom coughed. "But if the magic in *The Book of Charms* isn't rewritten, then the spells protecting the museum will fail. You said it yourself, Gideon. The Flame has chosen these five apprentices for their magical talents. We must assist them in every way. I propose you let me assess their magical talents so we can make an informed decision."

"I agree with Orpheus," said Brown. "If they have special gifts, then they should be encouraged."

"Very well," said Graves. "You may assess their magical ability."

"Excellent," said Gloom. "I will begin immediately. I must confess that Archie Greene is the one who interests me most."

Archie felt the color rise to his cheeks. There was a sound of people standing up.

"They're coming out," whispered Rupert. "Quick, let's get out of here!"

CHAPTER 8

Orpheus Gloom

"You are to report to the Scriptorium," Old Zeb informed Archie when he arrived at the Mending Workshop the next day.

Bramble, Thistle, Rupert, and Arabella were already there.

"What do you think he'll test us on?" asked Arabella anxiously.

"Who knows?" said Rupert. "But I imagine he will want to see if we have what it takes to write magic."

"We wouldn't have the Firemarks if we didn't," reasoned Archie, trying to sound upbeat. "And maybe we will learn something useful from the tests. Gloom does work for the Royal Society of Magic, after all. He must be pretty knowledgeable."

"Good thinking, Arch," said Thistle. "If we ask the right questions, Gloom will tell us what we need to do to write magic."

"But what if one of us turns out to be a darchemist?" said Arabella, voicing Archie's deepest fear.

The question hung awkwardly in the air.

As they waited outside, they heard voices coming down the stairs from the direction of Hawke's office.

"The Scriptorium has been neglected. It is time the magical world regained its confidence," said Gloom.

"I'm still not convinced it's safe for the apprentices to write magic," Hawke said. "I wish you'd wait until I had a chance to find out what's attacking the museum's defenses. I fear we are playing into the hands of the enemy."

"Nonsense," said Gloom. "We must embrace our heritage, not shy away from it. We have been hiding in the shadows for too long because we had no magic writers. The return of the Golden Circle Firemarks signals a new start. I think if you had your way, Gideon, I wouldn't be holding the assessments at all!" Gloom continued. "But the world needs magic now more than ever. Where's your ambition, man?"

"Ambition," muttered Hawke. "It was reckless ambition that led to magic being banned."

"Yes, but that's because Grey wasn't nurtured properly. That's why we must help these children, guide them in the right direction so that they don't make the same mistake."

"Grey had talent and he had ambition," continued Gloom. "It wasn't just writing magic that interested him. Look at his experiments with magical art. He was a brilliant painter, too."

"Grey was irresponsible," said Hawke. "He thought he knew more about magic than the Elders—and look where it led! It is because of him that magic was discredited and his friends were all—"

At that moment the two men turned the corner and saw the five apprentices waiting. Hawke fell silent. The children shot nervous glances at one another. What was he about to say? What had happened to Grey's friends? What was the secret that no one wanted them to know?

Katerina appeared from the direction of the Great Gallery.

"Ah, Katerina," said Gloom. "Glad you could join us. Your knowledge of the Magisters could be very valuable."

"Is this the Scriptorium?" Katerina asked excitedly,

gazing at the burnished oak doors.

Gloom smiled. "Yes, my dear," he said. "It is an exact replica of the original Scriptorium at the Great Library of Alexandria, where the great books of magic were written. This is the place where one day they will be rewritten and history will be remade."

Entering the room with the other apprentices, Archie felt a twinge of excitement and anticipation. As they stepped over the threshold, torches on the wall magically lit themselves and blazed to light the room. Thistle and Katerina gasped, but Archie had seen it before.

He had been inside the Scriptorium three times. Once when Bramble was showing him around the museum for the first time, and twice when he had entered *The Book of Yore* to find out about the past. The second time had almost ended in disaster when he'd become trapped by the fire inside the Great Library of Alexandria and had had to be rescued by Gideon Hawke.

Gloom smiled to himself. "Ah," he breathed. "The old magic stirs!"

In the center of the room, two rows of desks were shrouded in white dust sheets. More dust sheets were draped down the wall, concealing what lay beneath.

Whenever Archie entered the Scriptorium, he felt he

was trespassing on its stillness. That feeling came back to him strongly now. He felt a sudden sense of loss, as if the room itself was still grieving for something or someone.

He tried to put it to the back of his mind. He was there for a reason: to discover the secrets of writing magic. If he could do that, then the Alchemists' Club could rewrite *The Book of Charms* and dispel the shadow hanging over the museum.

Gloom saw his wistful look. "A great sadness lies on this place," he said. "It mourns the passing of the great magic writers of old."

He strode along the aisle between the rows of desks, running his fingers excitedly over their shrouded forms.

"When Barzak set fire to the Great Library of Alexandria and corrupted the magical books, there was nothing our ancestors could do except try to preserve them until they could be restored to their former glory."

He uncovered one of the desks, letting the dust sheet slither to the ground.

"By some miracle the contents of the original Scriptorium survived the fire. These are the very same desks where the old magic writers practiced their craft and the great books of magic were written. The desks were brought here from Alexandria. Look—you can still see the scorch marks from the fire.

"But by then there were no great magic writers left to use them. The last of the Magisters founded the museum and wrote the spells that have protected it all these years. And then something remarkable happened—Fabian Grey and his group of apprentices emerged with the Golden Circle Firemark. They squandered their opportunity. But now we have another chance in you.

"Ambition," he said. "Aspiration. These should be our watchwords. We must seize this moment—otherwise the museum and all it stands for will come to nothing.

"Here in this place the most precious books are stored." He gestured to a wooden podium where a large book with a brown leather cover was displayed. "*The Book of Yore* contains the history of magic," he said, shaking his head sadly. "It is a proud history, but we have forgotten the achievements of the past."

Katerina was staring at a glass dome at the far end of the room. "Are they what I think they are?" she said, gazing at the books inside.

"They are indeed," Gloom said. "Come up here so you can get a better view."

He led her up some stairs to a raised wooden platform. "Behold the Books of Destiny," he said dramatically. "*The

Book of Prophecy contains predictions about the future of magic," he said, indicating a gray book that was closed. "And that," he added, nodding at the very large open book, "is *The Book of Reckoning*. It keeps the tally between life and death."

The open book was the size of a table and raised up at an angle of forty-five degrees so that its pages were visible. Suspended in its center was an ornate crystal hourglass. The hourglass was protected by a silver case, which formed part of the spine. The pages of the book were shaped around it so that it could be seen even when the book was open.

A blue quill floated in the air just above its open pages. It was a magic quill from a Bennu bird, and it was constantly updating the names and dates. *The Book of Reckoning* recorded every birth and death in the magical realm.

Katerina was gazing at the books in wonder. Archie smiled to himself. He had had the exact same reaction when he first saw the Books of Destiny.

Archie glanced at the silver hourglass. It kept a tally of the time that was left until the books in the museum released their magic into the world. According to legend, that day would mark either the beginning of a new

Golden Age of Magic or the start of another Dark Age.

The last time the sand had moved, it had been a warning that the Greaders were plotting to steal *The Book of Souls*. Archie was relieved to see that the hourglass was still. He noticed that a third book had been placed inside the glass dome with the others.

Katerina interrupted his thoughts. "Is that *The Book of Charms*?" she asked, gazing with fascination at the most recent addition.

"Erm, yes," confirmed Gloom. "The elders have put it there for safekeeping. The glass dome is sealed with a guardian spell." Gloom's face turned suddenly troubled. "Although I suppose that even that will lose its strength as *The Book of Charms* fades."

"Then it is *The Book of Charms* that is the key to everything," said Katerina. "It is what protects the museum from attack."

She gestured at the Books of Destiny. "We must look to the future. We must develop the next generation—our generation." She paused. "You have the Golden Circle Firemark, so one of you will be the one to reclaim the place of magic in the world!"

"Quite so," exclaimed Gloom. "And that is why, despite the objections of some at the museum, I have brought you here today. I hope it will inspire you to achieve your full potential. It was in this very room that the last generation of magic writers honed their special gifts."

What Gloom didn't know was that the Alchemists' Club had already been re-formed. Archie caught a sideways glance from Arabella. Rupert nudged Bramble, and Thistle looked at his feet. Archie wondered what he'd got them all into.

"They were the most naturally gifted apprentices who ever worked at the museum," Gloom continued, tugging one of the dust sheets from the wall to reveal a large painting.

It was a picture of five young people in their late teens. There were three young men and two young women, all sitting at a table. The men wore black tunics with white collars, and the women wore long gowns pulled in tight at the waist. On the table in front of them was a black quill and a flask containing a golden liquid.

Two of the men and both of the women were facing the front and smiling. But the young man at the end of the table was turning away. Despite his youth, he had a streak of white running through his dark hair and appeared to be pointing at an open door at the back of the room. The man had his head turned toward it so that his expression was hidden. A sign beneath said THE ALCHEMISTS' CLUB, 1665.

Gloom stepped back to admire it. "It is the only picture we have of them," he said. "Grey painted it himself. They say it contains a prophecy about the future of magic."

With a flourish, he pulled off the other dust sheet to reveal a wooden plaque.

The Alchemists' Club, founded 1662
Fabian Grey
Braxton Foxe
Felicia Nightshade
Angelica Ripley
Roderick Trevallen

Beneath it was the Golden Circle symbol:

CHAPTER 9

Book Hauntings

Archie was convinced that there was something the elders still weren't telling them. The newly re-formed Alchemists' Club had decided to forge ahead with their own research.

Mudberry's *A Beginner's Guide to Magic* was a good starting point, Archie decided. Once again, it didn't let him down.

He found an entry for Azoth. The page was worn. It had obviously been read and reread many times.

AZOTH: a magical compound highly prized by alchemists. It is one of the three requirements for writing new magic, the other two being the Golden

Circle Firemark and an enchanted quill, made from
a feather given freely by a magical creature. The
ancient magic writers wrote their master spells with
Azoth because of its long-lasting properties. It can also
extend the life expectancy of mortals. The symbol for
Azoth is the caduceus.

＿＿＿

Arabella had been busy doing some research of her own
about the dangers involved with writing new magic. She
was working in the Supernatural Magic Department and
had access to Feodora Graves's study, which was located
in the North Gallery. Arabella had invited the other four
apprentices to meet her there that lunchtime, to share
what she had discovered.

Thistle, meanwhile, had been reading up on the different departments in *Magical Places to Visit*. He had it
open now and was looking at it as they walked.

"Katerina is right about Grey having a secret laboratory," he informed Archie and Bramble as the three
cousins made their way up a flight of marble stairs con-
necting the Great Gallery with the North Gallery. "Listen
to this:

"The locations of some magical places remain mysteries.
Among the most intriguing is the secret laboratory

of Fabian Grey. Grey is known to have carried out
magical experiments while still an apprentice at the
Museum of Magical Miscellany. It is believed that it
was here that he first discovered the secret to making
the magical substance Azoth. The exact location of
the laboratory remains unknown, but it is thought to
be somewhere within the museum. Grey's notebook
containing the formula for Azoth has also never been
found."

"Imagine if we could find it!" said Archie. "Maybe Grey left some clues there about how to make Azoth. Or even a secret stash of it!"

They passed through an arched doorway with a smiling skull above it, the symbol for Supernatural Magic. In front of them they could see a staircase that gave off an eerie light in the gloom. This was called the Pale Staircase. Flaming torches were set in brackets shaped like the clawed hands of grotesque beasts, and the balustrades had skulls carved into them, their mouths fixed in hideous grins.

The dark walls of the staircase were covered with runes and other magical designs that looked like they had been drawn with chalk and gleamed in the murky half-light.

They climbed the stairs until they reached the first landing, where Rupert was waiting for them.

"Hurry up," he said. "We haven't got long. Arabella says that Graves will be back soon.

"It's this way," he added, indicating a dingy hallway that led off from the main staircase. Behind them the stairs continued to rise into the shadows above.

The hallway ended in another arched doorway. Two demon-headed gargoyles stood outside as if on guard.

"Nice gargoyles!" joked Archie.

"Technically, they aren't gargoyles, they're grotesques," said Thistle, referring to *Magical Places to Visit*. "Gargoyles are decorative water spouts. These are grotesques because they are freestanding."

"Whatever they are, they don't look very friendly," replied Archie. "Look at the size of their claws!" He remembered how the Bookend Beasts, the two great stone griffins that had once guarded the Great Library of Alexandria, had turned from stone into flesh and blood in front of his eyes.

"Come on," said Rupert. "This place gives me the creeps. I don't want to be here any longer than necessary. Give me the Mythical Menagerie any day!"

Three-quarters of the way up the door was a brass

door knocker with a heavy brass ring. Rupert gave it a loud rap.

"Come in," said a voice from the other side.

The four apprentices stepped inside. They found themselves in a high-ceilinged chamber that resembled a Gothic crypt. There was a flagstone floor, and a wooden bench like a church pew to sit on.

Arabella watched them file into the room. She was sitting behind a desk, which had magical symbols carved into it and clawed feet. Scented candles burned, casting shadows on the wall. Some old books were piled on the floor at her feet. Archie, Thistle, Bramble, and Rupert sat down on the wooden bench.

"It's as cold as a tomb in here," muttered Thistle to Archie, pulling up his collar as they took their places.

"I think that's the idea," whispered Archie.

"Well, she could have lit a fire or something. How are we supposed to learn anything when we're shivering?"

"Don't be so pathetic," said Arabella. "Now, we haven't got long, so let's get on with it."

She said the oath. "I, Arabella Ebony Ripley, swear allegiance to the Alchemists' Club. I promise to do all I can to restore magic to its former glory.

They carried on down the line until they had all

repeated the pledge. On the desk in front of Arabella was a book entitled *Working with Spirits: A Beginner's Guide to the Supernatural World*, by Feodora Graves.

"Don't keep us in suspense," said Thistle, shivering. "What have you found out?"

"According to Graves, Supernatural Magic is the most powerful of the three. It's also the most dangerous. When you write magic, it's important to know which sort you are using. Darchemists work with Supernatural Magic. The Terrible Tomes are all books of Supernatural Magic."

She paused, her eyes roving around their faces.

"Supernatural Magic uses the power of dead spirits. Ghosts, ghouls, genies, demons, vampires, werewolves, banshees, zombies, golems, wraiths—you get the gist."

Bramble raised her eyebrows. "Well, that all makes sense," she said. "So what's the big deal?"

"Well," said Arabella. "The problem is that when people are first learning to write magic, they may not know which source they are using. You see, the spirits will use any trick. So an unwary alchemist might think they are writing magic using Natural Magic, only to discover they have been writing dark magic."

"Oh," said Archie, swallowing hard. "That does put

a different light on things. So how can we tell the difference?"

"That's what I'm going to show you," said Arabella, "if you give me half a chance. Most of the problems with unintended darchemy come from book hauntings.

"A book is haunted when a spirit is bound to it," she continued matter-of-factly. "Book hauntings are especially problematic if you don't know what sort of spirit you're dealing with. So I am going to show you what to look for.

"Most haunted books contain book ghasts," added Arabella. "They're unfulfilled dreams or promises."

She selected two books from the pile at her feet. "I'll need two volunteers."

"Just get on with it," sighed Thistle.

"For that, you can be the first one," said Arabella, her thin lips twitching into the faintests of smiles. "And Archie, you can be my other victim—I mean volunteer."

The two boys reluctantly stepped forward.

Arabella handed them a book each. "One of these two books is haunted," she said. "But which one?"

Archie regarded the book in his hand dubiously. Thistle shrugged.

"Exactly. There is no obvious way of telling just by looking at them," Arabella continued. "But there are some telltale signs if you know what to look for.

"The first and most obvious test is the temperature. If a book contains a spirit, it is likely to be a different temperature from the books around it. Generally, it will be cold—like the grave. But it could be hot.

"What temperature are the two books I gave you?"

"This one is like ice," said Thistle, touching the book's cover with his fingertips.

"So is this," confirmed Archie.

"That's because the room is cold."

"You're not kidding," breathed Thistle, who had put the book down and was rubbing his hands together to try to keep them warm.

Arabella arched an eyebrow at him in irritation.

"The second clue is smell," she said. "Supernatural Magic has the odor of decay. It smells like something rotting. So, what do our two books smell of? Go on," she urged, "smell them!"

Thistle reluctantly put his nose to his book. "Ugh!" he said. "It reeks of old parchment."

"I like the smell of parchment," said Arabella. "But it doesn't suggest anything supernatural. And yours, Archie?"

Archie placed his nose to the book's cover and immediately caught a whiff of something nasty—ammonia mixed with a sweet, sickly smell that made him gag. He pulled a face.

"It smells like something crawled inside and died!" he said.

"Which is precisely what happened," said Arabella. "This book is haunted—in this case by the book ghost of a magician from the time of the bubonic plague. He thought he'd invented a magical cure for the disease but discovered he hadn't when he ended up dead one day."

She took the book from Archie and flipped the cover open. A gray specter reared up from the book. It loomed over her, a tall, ghostly figure of a man in a long fur-trimmed coat and round pillbox hat.

"I have it this time! 'Tis a tincture of cow's dung and vinegar that will cure all known ills!"

Arabella turned to the ghost. "That's enough, Bartholemus Brandy," she said, in a commanding voice.

The specter crumpled and slid back inside the pages of the book.

"How did you do that?" asked Rupert, impressed.

Arabella tossed her head. "The supernatural comes very naturally to me! Besides, I've seen Graves do it. I can control the spirit because I know its name," she explained. "Remember that. Don't go writing spells if you don't know where they come from!

"Book ghasts are generally more pathetic than dangerous," she continued. "Most are trapped by their own misery. But book ghouls are a different matter. They're malevolent spirits waiting for a chance to come back into the world."

"What's that about book ghouls?" said Feodora Graves, walking into the room. "And what are you doing in my study?"

"I was just showing them your book," said Arabella, quickly joining the others.

"I see," said Graves suspiciously. "Well, now we have work to do, so I think the rest of you should be getting back to your own departments."

She paused as if deciding whether to say more. "There has been another Greader attack," she said. "It happened last night. Someone broke into the Royal Society of Magic and tried to steal their supply of Azoth. Fortunately, whoever it was wasn't unsuccessful."

~

That night at the Foxes' in Houndstooth Road, the conversation among the three cousins was dominated by the latest Greader attack.

"It can only mean one thing," said Archie. "Someone is trying to write magic."

"Yes," agreed Thistle. "But who?"

"Gloom is from the Royal Society," mused Archie. "Perhaps it's him?"

"But he wouldn't need to break in," said Bramble.

"Unless he wanted to throw suspicion off himself," said Thistle. "Anyway, why is he still at the museum? I thought he was just there to oversee the book fayre."

"He's a magic assessor," said Archie. "I think he wanted to assess our magical abilities from the start. And now he's got his chance."

"What's he assessing us for, anyway?" asked Thistle.

"To see if we can write magic," said Bramble. "It has to be."

"Well, I've got my first assessment tomorrow," said Archie. "So I guess I'll find out."

CHAPTER 10

The Whispering Book

The next day was Monday. When Archie arrived at the Scriptorium for his assessment, he found the door unlocked and went inside. The torches blazed as usual, illuminating the room with a golden aura.

Archie felt its sadness again and wondered whether he was intruding on its sorrow. But a room didn't have feelings, surely? He looked around.

Something about the room was different. For a moment he couldn't work out what it was, but then he realized that some more of the dust sheets had been removed to reveal a row of desks. They were each raised at a forty-five degree angle, with a high bench.

Archie reached out his hand and stroked the first desk. He felt a sense of excitement mixed with sadness. He closed his eyes and tried to imagine the original Scriptorium at the Great Library of Alexandria, buzzing with life and energy.

"You can feel it, can't you?" said a voice. Archie jumped. His eyes snapped open. Orpheus Gloom was studying him closely.

"The raw power of magic!" enthused Gloom. "I'm not talking about old magic preserved in books and artifacts, Archie. I'm talking about new magic being created. The air in here is thick with it. These desks have witnessed the act of creation itself! It's burned into them," he added, stroking one of the desks. "It's in their very fabric, written into the grain of the wood!"

"Yes, I suppose it is," said Archie, his eyes wide. He could feel the energy Gloom was talking about. Something deep inside him was stirring. Some primal force was starting to assert itself. He could feel his curiosity growing. He felt exhilarated but wary at the same time.

Gloom's eyes were fixed on him. "It's nothing to fear, you know, Archie."

Archie looked away. It was easy for Gloom to say that. He didn't have the forks on him! Nor did he have the

Golden Circle Firemark. Sometimes Archie wondered what his life would be like if he'd never heard of magic or the museum. He smiled to himself. Boring! That was the answer. But he felt the weight of responsibility on his shoulders. It was a lot to carry.

Deep down, too, Archie knew that what he feared most was himself. He was frightened by the thought that he might make the wrong decision when the time came. Who knows, maybe he had already made the wrong decision when he'd persuaded the others to re-form the Alchemists' Club. It had seemed so clear that they needed to rewrite *The Book of Charms* to save the museum.

But that was before they knew anything about a curse. He wondered whether the appearance of the raven and its warning was linked to his decision. It was not a very cheering thought.

Gloom opened his briefcase and removed a large note-book, which he placed on one of the uncovered desks.

"Now then, let's make a start," he said. "Take a seat."

Archie was about to sit down at the first desk, but he hesitated. He felt a strange reluctance.

"Come along, now," said Gloom, taking out a blue-tinted Imagining Glass and waving his hand impatiently. "Any of the desks will do."

Archie tried the next desk, but again it didn't feel right. He couldn't put his finger on it, but he didn't feel comfortable there. It was as if he was sitting in someone else's place. He glanced along the row. All were uncovered except for the one at the end, which was still draped in a dust sheet. Archie felt drawn to it. He tugged at the dust sheet and it fluttered to the ground.

He sat down.

"Welcome, Archie Greene," whispered a gentle voice. "You have chosen well."

Archie was taken aback. Had the desk just spoken to him? He gave it a curious look and glanced at Gloom. The magic assessor still had his nose in his briefcase and didn't appear to have heard the voice. Archie shook his head to clear it. He'd encountered plenty of magical objects at the museum, but only books had spoken to him before. It must be a book, he thought.

The voice spoke again. "The spells that keep the museum safe are very old. They are growing weak. Only you can protect the museum from the darkness."

Archie scanned the room. The only books he could see were *The Book of Yore* on its podium and the three books inside the glass dome. Could one of them be talking to him?

"Who are you?" he whispered, keeping his voice low so that Gloom wouldn't hear.

"You will know in time. I mean you no harm. But there are others who can't be trusted. Take care, Archie Greene."

Gloom looked up to see Archie seated at the far end of the row.

"What are you doing all the way down there?"

Archie shrugged. "You said to pick any desk."

"So I did," said Gloom thoughtfully. "Interesting that you should pick that one. It was Fabian Grey's desk."

Archie felt his heart quicken. The palms of his hands were suddenly sweating. He had been drawn to the desk. Was he destined to follow in Grey's footsteps? He glanced at the Books of Destiny. But the voice was silent.

Gloom opened his notebook. "Right, then. Tell me about this special book whispering talent of yours, Archie."

Archie felt suddenly awkward. "Well, I can hear magical books talking. But it's not all the time."

Gloom's eyebrows bristled with interest. "And how many times has this happened?" he asked, scribbling in his notebook.

Archie shrugged. Gloom looked up. "Come along, Archie, you've got to help me here," he said. "I can't assess your magical ability if you don't tell me everything."

Archie thought for a moment. "Well, it's happened quite a few times." He wondered whether he should tell Gloom that it had just happened again. But since he didn't know where the voice was coming from, he decided to keep it to himself.

"More than ten?" asked Gloom eagerly.

Archie nodded.

"So you can hear them, and they can hear you? I mean, they respond to your commands?"

Archie thought about how he had been able to release the warlock Barzak from *The Book of Souls*. "Well . . . yes, I suppose so. Sometimes, at least."

Gloom looked up sharply. "Fascinating," he said, still scribbling. "And has it happened recently?"

"Yes," said Archie. "Very recently." *About a minute ago,* he thought.

Gloom seemed to sense that Archie was holding something back. He gave him a searching look.

"I understand that you consulted *The Book of Yore*?"

Archie glanced at the large brown book at the far end of the room. "I asked it about what happened to my parents," he said.

All he knew about his family was the vague story

that Granny Greene had told him, that they had been victims of a cross-Channel ferry disaster. When he had first arrived in Oxford, Loretta had given him some of his father's books and photographs, but he knew almost nothing about his mother except her name—Amelia.

When he had asked *The Book of Yore* about his parents, it had shown him scenes from much earlier in the history of magic. It was all very confusing.

"It showed me Barzak trying to open the Terrible Tomes and the fire at the Great Library of Alexandria." He felt a shiver run up his spine at the memory. "I was trapped in the fire, until Gideon Hawke rescued me."

"I see," said Gloom. "So Hawke entered *The Book of Yore* as well?"

"No, he used a Book Hook to save me," said Archie. "I realize now that what I did was foolish."

"Foolish, yes," mused Gloom, looking up from his notes. "But also very brave, if I may say so. The fact that you managed to escape in one piece indicates magical ability as well as luck," he added, making another note. "But next time you may not be so fortunate."

"Next time? I didn't think apprentices were allowed to consult the Books of Destiny."

"Hmmm," said Gloom. "Well, strictly speaking, they

aren't. But I don't think we need concern ourselves with such petty rules, do we? After all, we are the future of magic, and we should not be limited by the mistakes of the past. Progress—that is the drum we march to, eh, Archie?"

Archie's mind was in a whirl. Gloom was very different from the other museum elders. He was concerned with moving forward, not staying stuck in the past. Archie felt inspired.

"Well, if you say it's all right . . ."

"Good," said Gloom. "But you will need some protection. I'm talking about magical devices—artifacts, magical paraphernalia, that sort of thing. Old Zeb mentioned a Keep Safe from John Dee?"

Archie's magic pendant was on its silver chain around his neck as usual. "I have this," he said.

"Ah, yes," said Gloom reverentially, "the Emerald Eye. I've heard of it. It's famous in the magical realm."

Gloom gazed at the green crystal. His fingers twitched as if he longed to take it, but he merely smiled.

"It is a beautiful object," he said admiringly. "Powerful, too. And to think of all the people Dee could have given it to, he chose you. Did he explain why?"

"He told me it would protect me," Archie said. "And that I would need it. But he warned me never to use it to see my own destiny—that's all. There wasn't much time for long explanations."

"No, I don't suppose there was," muttered Gloom thoughtfully. "Well, Archie, the Emerald Eye has many magical properties, which will be magnified in the hands of a book whisperer. It will protect you from magical books, even the dark ones, as long as you don't look directly at them. And it will preserve your spirit—allowing your retro-specter to wander.

"Your retro-specter is the shadow of your soul, but it is not the real thing," he explained, seeing the blank look on Archie's face. "It can safely enter a Drawing Book, for instance, without putting you in danger. As long as the Emerald Eye is safe, then no harm will come to you. All you have to do is grasp the crystal and pronounce your magical name—the secret name your parents gave you. That will release your retro-specter, and it will remain until you say your magic name again. Then you will return to your body."

"Oh," said Archie, his face falling. "I don't think I have one of those."

Gloom regarded him steadily. "You have one, all right. Your parents would have seen to it. It could be a family name or nickname.

"One other thing: Has a magical creature ever presented you with a quill, by any chance?"

"No," said Archie.

"Oh well, just a thought," muttured Gloom. "And Archie, it would be best if you don't discuss what we have been talking about with the other apprentices. I can tell already that you have great magical talent, and that can be a source of envy.

"It was the same for Fabian Grey. His magical talents were extraordinary. Apparently he had a bibliographic memory. He could recall passages and spells from any magical book he'd ever seen.

"But he made people uncomfortable. They were jealous, you see. And of course he got carried away with the Alchemists' Club. And now his name has been blackened."

He shook his head again. "Such a talent, such a shame. You have a lot in common with him, Archie. He had the forks on him, too. If only he'd made different choices.

"Anyway, come and see me when you have remembered your magical name. I'm sure if you think hard enough, it will present itself. Magical names have a habit of doing that."

⟶

Archie was thoughtful for the rest of the day. He barely said two words to Old Zeb all afternoon. Gloom had given him a lot to think about.

What had gone wrong for Fabian Grey that night? Gloom had given Archie an idea about how he might find out. But first he needed to discover his magical name, and that felt like looking for a very small needle in a very large haystack.

CHAPTER 11

The Mythical Menagerie

The next day after they had finished their apprentice-ship duties, Rupert had arranged to show the others the Mythical Menagerie, where he worked. Archie, Bramble, Thistle, and Arabella went into the West Gallery and through a door marked with a lightning bolt striking a tree, the symbol for Natural Magic. They climbed a wooden staircase to the second floor.

Rupert was waiting for them. He opened a heavy oak door and stepped inside. "Welcome to the Mythical Menagerie," he said with a wide grin on his face.

Ahead of them was a long, dark passageway, lit by lanterns casting a golden light. There were animal pens on either side, and they could sense creatures inside them moving around.

The first thing that hit Archie was the smell. The aroma of manure and straw reminded him of a farmyard. He half expected to hear chickens squawking and pigs grunting. But the sounds coming from the menagerie were very different.

He thought he heard a whinny, but it didn't sound like any horse he'd ever heard before. It had a musical quality to it that he could have listened to for hours. There were other odd, unidentifiable animal noises: snuffling, flapping, and squeaking. In the background, too, something bellowed. Most alarming of all was a deep, throbbing growl like a very powerful engine.

"It's feeding time," said Rupert cheerfully. "You can help if you like. Grab a bucket and follow me."

Some wooden buckets were lined up in a row by the door. The poor light meant it was hard to see what was inside them. Rupert picked up the first one and started to move down the row of pens. The other children grabbed a bucket each and followed.

Inside the first pen were some small animals that looked like guinea pigs. "Snufflings," said Rupert. "They're very friendly."

He opened the low gate and stepped inside. The small creatures gathered around him, nuzzling his toes affectionately. He took a handful of grain from his bucket and scattered it on the ground. The snufflings put their heads down and snuffled around to find the food.

"They're very sweet," said Bramble, "but they don't look very magical."

"You'd be surprised," said Rupert.

Just then, Thistle stepped into the pen, and a snuffling that was grazing nearby suddenly vanished. One moment it was there, the next it was gone.

"Where did it go?" asked Thistle.

"Snufflings have an unusual way of protecting themselves," said Rupert. "They secrete a special invisibility enzyme, which allows them to disappear if they sense danger."

At that moment the snuffling reappeared and nuzzled Thistle's foot.

"He's decided you're not a threat after all," said Rupert, throwing a handful of grain toward the little creature. "I think he likes you! Come on," he said, shooing them out of the pen and closing the gate.

"Desmond is next," he said, moving to the next pen. "He's a dodo."

The children heard a honking sound, and a curious-looking bird with a large bill and short legs waddled into sight.

"I thought that dodos were extinct," said Arabella.

"Shhh, don't tell Desmond," said Rupert. "He doesn't know. Throw him a couple of fish," he added, gesturing to Arabella's bucket.

"And here are the dryads," he continued, indicating a thickly wooded area behind a gate. "They're tree nymphs. Hello, Oak," he called, waving.

At first the other children couldn't see anything. "Where is it?" asked Archie, squinting at the branches of an oak tree.

"There," said Rupert, pointing. "See it now?"

They could make out a pixie-like creature wearing the top of an acorn on his head.

"And there's Elm and Ash," he said as two other dryads lowered themselves from their trees to get some food.

"They eat nuts and berries," he said. "There's some in that bucket you're carrying, Bramble."

Bramble held out a handful of red berries and peanuts. The dryads approached her shyly and then darted forward to take them from her.

The next pen was covered with wire mesh and had a

tall gate with blacked-out glass. The children could hear a flapping sound like metal wings.

"Stymphalians," said Rupert. "They're man-eating birds with poisonous dung. I think we'll pass on them."

"Not something your average pet shop would have, then!" said Archie.

"No, probably not," said Rupert, laughing. "They're not really house pets!"

"Can we see them?" asked Thistle, trying to peer through the darkened glass.

"Best not to," said Rupert. "A Stymphalian can kill you with one look in the eye or by breathing on you. We have to wear blindfolds to feed them. The only thing that's immune to them is a snuffling."

"Fair enough," said Thistle, rapidly moving on to the next pen.

"Over there are the golden hinds and the satyrs," said Rupert, indicating two larger pens. "And that's Simon, the red-bellied salamander that ate my cuff links," he added, pointing to a large creature with a pinkish tinge. He was as big as a full-grown pig.

"No jewelry for you today, Simon," he said. "You're on a diet." He took the bucket that Bramble was carrying and emptied it under the gate.

As they watched him, the salamander changed color from pink to yellow and then to an angry red.

"Uh-oh," said Rupert. "He's about to flame. Watch out!"

The children dodged to one side just as the salamander opened his mouth and a flame shot out, blasting the metal door.

They could hear the sound of snorting coming from the next pen. The gate had heavy iron bars. Staring angrily at them from inside was a creature with a very large head like a buffalo, with two very sharp horns and the body of a man.

"The Minotaur," said Rupert, as if this explained everything. "Always cross about something."

At that moment, the beast bellowed like they had heard earlier. He put his head down and charged at them. The children leaped backward as he crashed his horns into the gate, making the ground tremble.

"Good thing we had those bars reinforced," said Rupert. "He must be hungry." He threw something between the bars, and the snorting Minotaur picked it up and carried it off to the far side of his pen.

The children gave one another a look and raised their eyebrows.

"He doesn't seem very pleased to be here," said Archie.

"He's not," said Rupert. "But can you imagine the trouble he'd cause if we let him loose in Oxford?

"Come on," he added. "I want to show you my favorite."

This pen was much larger than the others. At first it appeared to be empty.

"Shhhhh," hushed Rupert, putting his finger to his lips. "Be quiet or you'll scare her."

"I can't see anything," said Arabella.

"Look, over there," he whispered.

And then they saw her—a magnificent white horse. She was standing so still, they hadn't seen her.

"She's a Pegasus," breathed Rupert. "The very last of her kind."

And as he said it, the beautiful animal trotted forward and broke into a canter. They could see two white-feathered wings folded upon her flanks. With a shock, Archie realized they were closed with a leather strap.

"If we're lucky, she might come a little closer," said Rupert. "But she's very shy."

He opened the gate and stepped into the pen. He made a whistling sound, and the creature's ears pricked up.

"Does she ever get a chance to fly?" asked Archie, watching the Pegasus trotting around in a circle.

Rupert shook his head sadly. "No, she hasn't flown since I've been working here. We have to keep her wings tied. Her pen isn't big enough, and it would be too dangerous to let her out of Mothballs. If someone saw her, they would try to catch her and put her in a zoo. She'd hate that—people staring at her all the time.

"That reminds me—when I had my assessment with Gloom, he was especially interested in the magical creatures with feathers," he added. "He asked if one of them had ever presented me with a quill."

"That's interesting," said Archie. "He asked me the same thing."

"Apparently, that's what happened with the original Alchemists' Club," said Rupert. "Each of the members had a quill from a different magical creature. Three of them are in the Scriptorium."

CHAPTER 12

Pudding Lane

The next meeting of the re-formed Alchemists' Club was that weekend. They still hadn't found anywhere better to meet, so they agreed to use the Scriptorium.

Despite racking his brain, Archie was none the wiser about his magical name. He had tried all the family names he knew, grasping the Emerald Eye and saying them out loud, including Granny Greene's first name, Gardenia, and the first names of both his parents, Alexander and Amelia.

He wasn't really sure what was meant to happen, but he was certain that he'd recognize the retro-specter spell if it worked. He had also tried his own name, Archibald, and the names of all the Foxes: Loretta, Woodbine, Bramble, and Thistle. In a moment of inspiration, he tried the name of the last librarian of Alexandria, Obadiah Greene. He had even tried the name of the Foxes' cat, Timothy, and Granny Greene's dog, Mr. Barker.

But he was about to get some unexpected help.

When Archie arrived, Rupert was already there, standing in front of the portrait.

"All right, Rupert?" he said.

Rupert jumped. "Erm, yes. Just looking at the picture. That's my ancestor, Roderick Trevallen," he said, pointing to a tall young man with dark hair. "I looked him up. He died young, not much older than I am now. An accident."

Archie could see there was a strong family resemblance with Rupert. He took a closer look at the other alchemists in the picture.

The girl on the right of the group stared back with cold gray eyes. She must be Angelica Ripley. The eyes ran in the family. Archie could see the likeness with Arabella. The man next to Angelica looked a bit like a younger version of Woodbine. He must be Braxton Foxe.

"That's Grey," said Rupert, "the one looking away, with the white streak in his hair. Apparently he had a shock that turned some of his hair white when he was still an apprentice at the museum."

Grey's hand was raised, pointing at the open door behind him. Something glinted in his other hand.

"What's he holding?" asked Archie.

"The golden Bennu quill," said Rupert. "It was the most powerful of all the enchanted quills. It disappeared with Grey."

Archie looked closer. He could just make out the shape of the quill.

He reached out toward the painting. He wasn't sure what he was expecting to happen, but when his fingers touched it, the painting was hard and unyielding.

"What are you doing?" asked Rupert in surprise.

"It was just an idea," said Archie, feeling a little foolish.

At that moment, the others arrived. The five of them stood around in a circle.

As usual the club meeting began with the oath. Bramble went first. They carried on around the circle until it was Archie's turn.

Archie closed his eyes. "I, Archibald Obadiah Greene, swear—"

At that moment he caught sight of *Magical Places to Visit*. Thistle had put the book down on one of the desks. It was open at the page where their grandfather had written his nickname, Gadabout. Wait a moment. Archie had an idea. Gloom had said that magical names were often nicknames that had been passed down in a family. Archie's grandfather had liked to explore. Perhaps Archie's parents had given their son his nickname as his magical name.

Reaching inside his shirt, he grasped the Emerald Eye. He felt it glow warm as he squeezed it in his hand. He closed his eyes and uttered a single word.

"Gadabout."

The crystal began to throb, and Archie felt the strangest sensation, as if he was slipping out of his body.

"Wow! That was weird," he cried, his eyes still closed. "Did you feel it, too? Bram?"

There was no reply. "Thistle?" Still nothing. "Rupert? Arabella?" He opened his eyes. They were talking as if nothing had happened.

Archie took a step toward Bramble. His movement left a trail of silvery light like phosphorescence. He stared at his hands, which were shimmering, ghostlike. As he turned he caught sight of himself, his hand still gripping the Emerald Eye. The spell had worked. He had released his retro-specter!

Archie glanced at his friends, chatting among themselves. As far as they were concerned, he was still there. The Archie they could see was smiling amiably but wasn't saying anything. None of the others seemed to have noticed the blank expression on his face.

Archie felt a thrill of excitement. He was doing magic! But now that he had cast the spell, what was he going to do with it? Luckily, he had already thought about that. If the re-formed Alchemists' Club was going to avoid the same mistake as the original Alchemists' Club, he needed to know what had happened on the night of the fire in Pudding Lane. This was his chance to find out.

Gloom had said that his retro-specter would protect him if he consulted *The Book of Yore*. Archie approached it and said in a clear voice, "What happened on the night that Fabian Grey caused the Great Fire of London?"

He heard the sandpaper voice he knew from when he'd consulted the book before.

"The past is gone," the voice said in a cracked whisper. "Those who disturb it cannot change it, but they may be changed by it."

"I will take that chance," he said.

The Book of Yore flipped open. Its pages turned as if the wind blew through them. Then the book slammed shut.

"Your page is marked," the voice said.

Archie opened the pages to where a bookmark had

appeared. A date was written at the top of the page: *2 September 1666*. Archie reached out to touch the page, but his hand passed straight through. There was a rushing sound in his ears, and he closed his eyes. Like smoke up a chimney, he was drawn into *The Book of Yore*.

———

When he opened his eyes, he found himself in a darkened street. There were terraced houses with candles burning in the windows. The air was thick with fog, and he could barely see three feet in front of him.

A bell clanged and a voice called out, "Ten o'clock and all's well!"

The town crier was making his evening patrol. His dark shape loomed out of the thick mist. Another man, wearing a dark blue cloak, approached from the opposite direction. Something about the second stranger gave Archie the oddest feeling. He felt the hairs on the back of his neck rise. It was as if he had seen him before but didn't know where.

"Excuse me," said the stranger. "I'm looking for Thomas Farrinor's shop in Pudding Lane."

"It's down there," said the town crier, pointing.

"Thanks. It's this wretched fog. I can't see a thing."

"If you ask me, it's unnatural," said the town crier. "It's

them mad magicians up to their tricks again. They use the baker's shop for their meetings."

So the Unready knew about the alchemists operating in London at that time. The man seemed suspicious, but it sounded as if ordinary people tolerated the magical realm. With a jolt, Archie realized that this was because it was before the Great Fire that led to the new Lores. It was still legal to practice magic. That was all about to change. Little did the night watchman or anyone else realize the significance of what was about to happen!

That very evening an event would alter the history of magic forever. And the name of the baker, Thomas Farrinor, would go down in Unready history as the one to blame.

Archie sniffed the air. He smelled sulfur and something sweet like vanilla. Amora.

The stranger pulled his cloak a little closer. Archie watched him vanish back into the fog. He felt a strange sadness as he did, an empty longing and sense of missing someone. He had a sudden desperate impulse to chase after him, but the figure had already vanished into the fog.

The town crier carried on with his nocturnal vigil, turning left into another lane, leaving Archie alone in the street. He sniffed the air again. As well as magic, he could smell something else—chocolate!

He followed the scent. It was coming from a building to his left. A sign above the window said QUILL'S COFFEE & CHOCOLATE HOUSE. JACOB QUILL, ESQ. Archie remembered that Quill's had started in London. This must be the original shop. He smiled to himself.

FRESH BREAD, said the sign on the shop next door. THOMAS FARRINOR, ROYAL BAKER, EST. 1646. Archie heard footsteps approaching.

At first he could not see anyone, but then the figure of a man in a scarlet cloak appeared out of the fog. Archie couldn't see his features clearly, but he recognized the white streak of hair from the painting. It was Fabian Grey.

Grey looked straight through him. Archie's retrospecter was no more than a shadow to him.

Grey approached the bakery, but as he did, the stranger who had spoken to the town crier loomed out of the mist. The two men talked briefly. The stranger handed Grey a note and disappeared back into the fog.

Grey read the note. He stood for a moment, thinking, and then he stuffed the piece of parchment into his pocket and opened the front door to the bakery. Archie watched as he disappeared down some stairs into the cellar. He slipped down the stairs behind Grey.

He found himself in a narrow, low-ceilinged passage-way. Grey had vanished. Ahead of him, a sliver of light spilled from under a doorway. Archie crept quietly up to the door and put his ear to it.

He could hear muffled voices. Kneeling down, he put his eye to the keyhole and looked into the cellar. He could see five shadowy figures.

Even in the poor light, Archie recognized them from the painting: Angelica Ripley, Felicia Nightshade, Roderick Trevallen, and Braxton Foxe. Grey had his back to Archie, but Archie could see the streak of white in his otherwise dark hair.

"Is everything ready?" Grey asked.

"Yes," said Felicia. "We have followed the instructions you gave us to the letter."

The cellar was larger than Archie had realized. In the center, five flaming torches had been placed in a circle. The five alchemists took up positions behind the flames, facing one another.

Grey addressed them. "Azoth is made of the four elements: water, earth, air, and fire. Each of you was given instructions to collect one of the four. Have you done as you were asked?"

The other four alchemists nodded. In the torchlight,

Archie could see that each held something in his or her hand. Grey opened his bag and took out a notebook and a crystal chalice.

"I will pass the chalice among you. Each of you must add your element in the correct order, starting with you, Braxton."

He passed the glass to Braxton Foxe, who held up a glass flask for all to see and poured in a liquid. "Water from on high: rain collected from the highest mountain in the Himalayas," he declared.

Braxton Foxe passed the chalice to Roderick Trevallen, who added a brown powdery substance. "Salt of the earth: soil from the crater of a volcano," he pronounced.

Angelica Ripley was next. She held up a tiny leather bellows and inserted its nozzle into the glass. "Air of innocence: the first breath from a newborn babe," she said as she squeezed the bellows, sending bubbles of air to mingle with the other ingredients.

"And now you, Felicia," said Grey.

Felicia Nightshade held up a glass flask containing some glowing embers. "Immortal fire: a light from the Flame of Pharos," she said, emptying the embers into the mixture.

"And finally," said Grey, "the secret ingredient that has eluded us so long, the essence of magic itself."

He sprinkled something into the mixture, a golden powder that glistened in the torchlight.

The solution flared, and the five torches all turned red.

In a loud, clear voice, Grey pronounced:

> *"Powers of the universe*
> *Drawn by Nature's right*
> *The moment of Creation*
> *All of magic's might."*

The solution began to seethe and boil. Suddenly, there was a roaring sound and a blinding flash. The liquid started to glow with a golden light.

"Behold," declared Grey, holding the glass aloft, "Azoth! Each of your quills must be dipped in it!"

Archie watched in awe as Grey took a golden quill from his bag and immersed its tip in the liquid. One by one the other alchemists produced their quills and did the same. Braxton Foxe went first, then Roderick Trevallen and Angelica Ripley. Archie could see the golden nibs glowing in the gloom.

Felicia Nightshade was last. In her hand she held a black quill, which she thrust into the glass chalice. Then she produced a black book from her bag and opened it.

"You cannot write magic yet," cried Grey. "It is too soon!"

"Nonsense," cried Felicia. Holding the quill firmly, she began to write in the book.

As she scribbled on the dry parchment, fiery letters began to appear in the air above her head. The other alchemists watched in hushed awe, and Archie gazed in wonder.

The air crackled with static electricity.

The fiery letters began to form into words. Black words.

In dark places where none may go

Grey stared at the dark letters in the air. "What is that book?" he cried.

Felicia seemed to be in a trance. The fiery letters above her head started to twist and writhe.

Shadows linger from long ago . . .

"It is *The Grim Grimoire*!" cried Grey. "Felicia, stop before it is too late!"

Felicia hesitated.

Archie heard another voice. It was high and mocking and sounded like fat spitting on a fire. "Finish the spell!"

it shrieked. It was coming from the *Grimoire*.

Felicia's hand began to move, but Grey snatched the black quill from her and tried to snap it in two. The quill bent but did not break.

The black letters began to unravel, scattering flaming fragments around the room.

"Noooooo!" cried Felicia. "You have interrupted the spell. The Unfinished Spell is incomplete."

The cellar was on fire now. The other alchemists stepped away from their torches. They were backing away toward the door.

Archie stared in horror at the events unfolding in the cellar. He had assumed that Fabian Grey was the reason for the accident. After all, he was the leader of the Alchemists' Club. But now it seemed that it had been Felicia. Was this Grey's great mistake—to trust his friends with the power of writing magic?

He could see Grey's despair. There was nothing he could do to stop the magical experiment from raging out of control. It had taken on a dark power of its own.

The black quill twitched in Grey's hand. Felicia snatched it away from him and began to write again. Her blank eyes stared straight ahead.

"If I cannot finish Hecate's spell, then I will use the

Grimoire's power to curse you all!" she roared.

The fiery letters that formed in the air were distorted, with misshapen letters, but they were still readable.

> *A curse be upon you*
> *And all those whose name*
> *Is marked out for greatness*
> *By the magical flame.*
> *When you seven times fifty*
> *Have passed round the sun*
> *Old scores shall be settled*
> *Or the spell be undone.*

"Felicia, no!" cried Grey. "What have you brought upon us?"

The cellar was in chaos now. The letters from the failed spell were setting fire to whatever they touched. As the flames threatened to engulf them, Angelica Ripley and Roderick Trevallen turned and ran to escape the fire. Archie stood aside as they sped past him and up the stairs.

"It's hopeless! You must save yourselves," cried Braxton Foxe as he, too, turned and ran for the door.

Flames had surrounded the black book, as if daring anyone to go near. Felicia was trying to reach it, but the flames were too fierce and beat her back. Grey stood motionless, transfixed by what was happening around him. He still had his back to Archie, but his shoulders had slumped like a broken man's. Felicia's look of triumph had turned to something else. Scorn. She seized the notebook and ran for the door.

With a final glance into the burning cellar, Archie sped up the stairs after the fleeing alchemists. The fire had begun to spread, and new shrieks from the neighbors answered the desperate cries of the alchemists. As Archie fought his way through the choking smoke, a man in a blue cloak, the stranger from earlier, passed him on the stairs, heading in the opposite direction toward the fire.

By the time Archie reached Pudding Lane, the bakery was ablaze. For a moment, he stood in the street and watched the tongues of flame as the breeze spread them to the adjacent houses. The street was filling with people abandoning their homes or coming to see what was going on.

"Gadabout," Archie whispered. He closed his eyes and felt himself being drawn back to the present day.

———

When he opened his eyes again, he was in the Scriptorium. He held up his hand. It shimmered and he knew he was still in his retro-specter.

His mind was reeling from what he had just seen. "Gadabout," he said, and his retro-specter evaporated like mist in sunlight as he sank into his own body.

The others were still talking as if he had never been away and no time had passed at all.

⌒

"Are you telling us they made Azoth?" asked Bramble later, when he told them what he'd seen in the cellar.

"Yes," said Archie, "I saw them mix it."

"That's amazing," said Bramble. "No one has been able to make Azoth in hundreds of years."

"But it all went wrong when they tried to write new magic," said Arabella. "I told you it was dangerous."

"No, it wasn't that," said Archie thoughtfully. "It was the book that Felicia Nightshade was using. She was writing dark magic."

"Are you sure?" asked Bramble.

"Certain," said Archie.

CHAPTER 13

The Black Door

The members of the re-formed Alchemists' Club were alarmed by what Archie had discovered. The curse meant they were in real danger. They had formed the club to try to save the museum, but they were beginning to realize that they might need saving themselves.

Elsewhere in the magical realm, the news was grim. There were reports of two more Greader attacks. A potions expert in Wales had been attacked at home and his house ransacked; and a magical bird collector who lived in the Highlands of Scotland had been murdered and his collection of feathers stolen. Amos Roach had been spotted near the scene on both occasions.

The news had hit Loretta and Woodbine hard. They were growing increasingly concerned about the safety of the children.

"Make sure you wear your Keep Safes at all times," Loretta told them. "And don't talk to any strangers."

To make matters worse, Woodbine had been called away. The details were sketchy. All the children knew was that Gideon Hawke had sent him on a secret mission. Neither Woodbine nor Loretta had said exactly what it was for, but there was mention of finding a book and tracing a family tree. More than that they would not say. But it meant that Woodbine would be away from home for a while. Archie and his two cousins speculated that it was Fabian Grey's notebook that Woodbine was searching for. All in all it made for a very unsettled feeling at 32 Houndstooth Road.

There was one piece of good news, but even that had a barb. Archie had been puzzling over the meaning of the riddle and thought he'd finally worked it out.

"It takes the earth a year to travel around the sun," he explained at the next meeting. "And seven times fifty is three hundred and fifty. So as the curse was made in 1666, it's due to return in three hundred and fifty years. That's . . . any time now!"

This made it even more vital that they find a way to write magic and lift the curse. Spurred on by this, the children had redoubled their efforts to find a new meeting place for the Alchemists' Club. They couldn't keep using the Scriptorium. It was already making the elders suspicious. Their last meeting had been interrupted three times—first by Graves, then by Gloom, and finally by Rusp, who had started patroling the museum at night, and had told them they had no business there and sent them packing.

They needed somewhere secret to conduct their experiments if they were to stand any chance of rewriting *The Book of Charms* in time.

When they weren't carrying out their apprentice duties, Archie and Thistle spent their time searching for Fabian Grey's laboratory. They had to be discreet, so they mostly confined their activities to the evenings when the museum was quieter. They used Thistle's curiosity compass to search for places with unusually high magical energy.

So far they had concentrated on the main museum. But they had decided they should widen their search to include the Aisle of White.

They chose Screech's day off and waited until Marjorie and Old Zeb had gone home. Then Archie used his key to let them into the shop. They spent an hour walking up and down the aisles between the bookcases, staring at the compass. The needle started spinning at one point, but their excitement turned to disappointment when it turned out to be a broom cupboard containing a mildly magic mop and feather duster.

At this point they were so desperate that they would have considered a cupboard. Unfortunately, this one was too small to fit five people, even after removing the mop and duster. They had found nothing since, but they hadn't given up hope.

"Let's try the Mending Workshop," suggested Archie. "I've got a key, and with Old Zeb out of the way, we'll have the place to ourselves."

They ducked through the velvet curtain at the back of the shop and walked along the passageway. Archie heard the magic books on the bookcase wishing him luck. To Thistle's bewilderment, he thanked them. Then he took a lantern from the shelf, and they hurried down the spiral stairs to the underground passage that led to the workshop.

At the bottom of the stairs, Thistle paused in the passageway outside the first arched door. "There's all sorts of magical energy coming from there," he said, looking at the compass in his hand.

"There would be," confirmed Archie. "That's the

enchanted entrance I told you about. I've used it a couple of times to get into the museum."

Thistle moved along to the second door. "And there," he said, indicating the blue door.

"That'll be the crypt," said Archie. "Best not to go in there. We don't want to disturb the Bookend Beast. Let's try the workshop."

He took a key from his pocket and unlocked the third door. They walked through the large workshop, but Thistle shook his head.

"Apart from the Word Smithy, there's nothing out of the ordinary," he said.

"That'll be the Flame," said Archie. "But we haven't tried over there yet," he added, pointing at a place in the workshop by the door.

Thistle took another reading from the compass. "That's more like it," he said. "There's a strong magical energy coming from somewhere."

His face creased into a frown. "That's odd, though. It's not coming from inside the workshop. It's coming from the passageway."

"It'll be the enchanted entrance or the crypt, then," said Archie, disappointed.

"No," said Thistle, stepping through the door into the corridor, "it's coming from the other direction.

What's up there? It looks like a door."

Archie felt a surge of excitement. The black door! Old Zeb had said it had been sealed centuries ago. Why hadn't he thought of it before? That would be about the same time as the Great Fire of London!

The two boys advanced down the passageway. Archie held up the lantern so they could see the door clearly. It was made from black oak, heavily reinforced with iron, and locked with a bolt and heavy chain.

Archie examined the lock, which was also black. "Wait here," he said, handing Thistle the lantern. "I'll be right back." He raced back to the workshop and checked the hooks where Old Zeb kept his keys. Next to the silver key for the enchanted entrance was a black key. By the look of the rust on it, it hadn't been used in many years. Archie grabbed it and tore back along the passageway.

"Hold up the light so I can see," he said. He fitted the black key into the lock. It turned with a hollow click. The two boys looked at each other, hardly able to breathe for excitement.

The door groaned on its hinges and they stepped inside, brushing through thick cobwebs and leaving a trail of footprints in the dust-covered floor. The air smelled stale from being shut up so long. There was an acrid aroma of burned chemicals and stale magic.

At that moment, a flame ignited in a sconce on the wall so they could see clearly. They found themselves in a long, low-ceilinged room. Rows of shelves displayed glass jars filled with murky solutions. Archie peered into one and pulled back when he realized that the black object suspended in the cloudy liquid was a perfectly preserved scorpion.

A long wooden bench dominated the room, with more glass flasks connected by a spaghetti jumble of rubber tubing. Several open books were scattered facedown along the bench, discarded years ago by someone too busy or preoccupied to close them. Some of their pages had been badly singed. Along the bench, too, were black scorch marks.

In one corner, an old dust sheet lay on the ground and paint speckled the floor and splashed up the walls. Someone had used the room as a studio. An inscription on a wooden plaque above the bench said: WE PLEDGE TO RESTORE MAGIC TO ITS FORMER GLORY.

Archie felt goosebumps. They had found it: Fabian Grey's laboratory!

The two boys raced off to tell the others. Half an hour later, all five members of the Alchemists' Club were standing in the laboratory, their faces flushed with excitement. Bramble picked up one of the discarded books on the bench.

"The Alchemy of Magic," she said, reading its spine. "Grey and the others must have used this place for their early experiments in writing magic. And by the look of those burn marks on the bench, some of them weren't a great success."

She pointed at five iron braziers stacked in one corner of the room. "I bet these are what made the scorch marks."

The others were nosing around the room. "Look at this," cried Rupert, pointing at something floating in one of the glass jars. "It's a tarantula."

"That's disgusting!" said Arabella, curling her lip at the sight of the huge hairy spider.

"Well," said Bramble brightly, "we've found our new meeting place, all right."

"But it's filthy!" moaned Arabella, pulling a face. She picked up a tiny set of leather bellows and examined them. "We could catch something."

"Let's hope it's not the plague," joked Thistle.

"It's nothing that a broom, some soapy water, and lots of elbow grease won't fix," replied Bramble cheerfully. "We'll have this place looking spic-and-span in no time."

The children set about cleaning the laboratory. Archie brought a broom from the Mending Workshop, and they used the mop from the cupboard in the bookshop. Rupert tore the dust sheet into strips so the others could help wipe away the grime. Then they set to work.

Even Arabella joined in with barely a grumble, using the feather duster from the broom cupboard to brush away the cobwebs on the ceiling. They tried not to disturb anything that looked like it might be an important clue, replacing all the glass jars exactly where they had found them. Archie and Thistle carefully collected the books, placing them in a neat pile at one end of the bench. At Archie's suggestion, they bookmarked the pages they were opened at just in case there were leads.

"What exactly are we looking for?" asked Arabella, checking the books on the bookshelves.

"Anything that could tell us how to make Azoth," said Archie, "especially Grey's notebook."

By the time they had finished, it was late. The place looked almost unrecognizable.

"There," said Bramble, wiping the last of the dust from the wooden plaque and straightening it on the wall. "The Alchemists' Club is back in business!"

"When shall we hold our first official meeting here?" asked Thistle.

Archie had a worrying feeling that there was no time to lose. "How about tomorrow?" he said.

"Tomorrow it is, then," said Rupert. "We'll meet here straight after we finish at the museum."

~

The next day dragged by. Archie watched the time, desperate for five o'clock, the time they finished work, to arrive. He made sure he was busy repairing a spell book when the old bookbinder was getting ready to leave. Archie offered to lock up the shop, and the old man gratefully accepted. As soon as Archie was sure everyone had left for the night, he took the black key, which he'd carefully replaced the night before, and hurried along the corridor.

He unlocked the black door and waited in the lab. He knew the other four were watching the shop from Quill's and would be along as soon as they saw the coast was clear. They arrived a few minutes later.

"I have some news," declared Arabella. "Katerina has agreed to show us some advanced alchemy. She was excited that we'd found Grey's lab."

The others exchanged glances. "You told her?"

"Of course," said Arabella. "She was the one who told us about it in the first place. And besides, she's dying to see it. She's been studying Grey for years."

"But what if she tells the elders?" asked Thistle.

"She won't," said Arabella. "I told her it was a secret."

"Did you tell her about the club?" asked Archie.

"No, of course not," said Arabella. "But she will be here any minute, so let's quickly say the oath."

They had just finished when the door opened and Katerina strode into the room carring a large bag. Her eyes were shining with emotion.

"I can't believe it!" she exclaimed. "Fabian Grey's laboratory. You found it! All these years, and it was right under our noses.

"And his books!" she cried, catching sight of where Archie and Thistle had neatly stacked the books from the bench. "And what are these?" She picked up a glass jar and held it up to peer into its murky interior.

"Everything must be cataloged," she said. "It is of huge interest for magical scholars like myself. We must make an inventory. Have you moved anything?"

"We tidied up a bit," said Bramble. "The place was pretty dirty."

"Ah," said Katerina, her blue eyes glistening in the torchlight, "but did you touch anything or take anything away?"

"You mean did we find any Azoth," Archie said. "The answer is no, we didn't."

"Yes, well, perhaps the formula is hidden here

somewhere among Grey's papers," said Katerina. "I can help you find it if you like. The elders don't need to know. I can say that I found Grey's notebook in the Archive."

She glanced around the room and shook her head as if she couldn't quite believe what she was seeing. "Now, Arabella asked me to show you some alchemy. I brought a few ingredients with me, and there might be some already here."

She plucked a jar from the shelf and examined the label. "Aha, powdered tortoiseshell. And that," she added, picking up another jar with what looked like a coiled snake in it, "is slow-worm skin. I think we have everything we need to make a slow potion. It will give you an idea of how to combine elements."

"This should be interesting," whispered Bramble. "Arabella says Katerina trained in alchemy at the Prague Academy of Magic."

"I've brought some equipment so you can all make your own potions," said Katerina. She took some things from her bag and placed them on the workbench with the two jars.

Archie peered at them. There were five glass containers shaped like test tubes but with wider flat bottoms, five pestles and mortars for crushing ingredients, and five long glass rods for stirring. In addition, she'd brought several shallow dishes.

In the first one were some green leaves; another contained dark blue berries.

Next to these, Katerina placed a glass phial containing a silvery liquid and a small dish of a gritty black substance. Away from the other ingredients was a taller container with an ornate silver stopper. Inside, a clear liquid sparkled.

Katerina was giving instructions. "I've measured out the ingredients very precisely. Get a flask each and divide up the thyme leaves equally among you. Then crush them with the pestle and mortar," she said, indicating the greenery in the first dish, "and put them in your flasks.

"We can use these to heat the solutions," she added, pointing at the braziers stacked in the corner. "Take one each." The children did as she told them, and Katerina poured something into each brazier and lit it with a match.

"That's it," she said, striding up and down behind them and inspecting the bookshelves as they carried out her instructions. "Put all the leaves in, Arabella. You don't want any thyme left over at the end.

"Careful, Rupert. I said crush them, not grind them!

"That's good, Archie. Just like that." Archie dropped the mashed-up thyme into the flask.

"Now add some of the melted glacier water."

Archie poured in some of the liquid, and the thyme

immediately started to dissolve. Katerina turned to watch Thistle.

"That's good, Thistle," she encouraged him. "Now, take the sloe berries and drop them in one at a time. You'll need five each."

There was a popping sound as one of the sloes that Arabella dropped into her flask exploded.

Katerina dodged out of the way as another sloe berry exploded in midair, squirting juice all over the floor.

"Steady, Arabella!" Katerina said. "This is a slow potion, not a Motion Potion!"

"Oops!" said Arabella, pulling a face as the potion bubbled up over the top of the flask and oozed down the side.

Archie's own potion wasn't going to plan either. Instead of dissolving as they were meant to, the sloe berries had clumped together on the surface like blue life buoys. At that moment, one of them shot into the air and exploded, shooting black juice all over him.

Katerina smiled and shook her head. "Archie, that's a disaster," she said. "When you make a potion, it's important that you combine the ingredients carefully in the correct order and at the right speed. Ah, Bramble, that's very good. I can see that we have one natural alchemist."

Bramble's potion had turned a dark shade of violet and was bubbling gently on the heat. The sloe berries had dissolved to leave a smooth, viscous liquid.

Bramble looked pleased at the compliment. Archie remembered the time when Bramble had made a Motion Potion to get them into the museum. She did seem to have a talent for it. Katerina was standing behind her now, watching as she stirred in the final ingredients.

"The rest of you, leave your own potions and watch what Bramble is doing."

Archie saw that Arabella had already abandoned her flask and was watching. He did the same.

"Okay, Bramble," said Katerina. "Now, add the tortoiseshell flakes—that's the brown powder—and the slow-worm skin. They are both slowing agents. Then, when you stir it, the slow potion will be ready, but before you do, I want to show you the antidote."

She indicated the dish with black powder on it. "That's quicksand. Watch as I mix it with some quicksilver and some rapids water to make a quickening potion. We'll need it to undo the effects of the slow potion."

Katerina poured the quickening potion into a cup. Then she returned her attention to Bramble, smiling as the final flakes of slow-worm skin dissolved.

"Now give it another good stir," she said.

Bramble did as she was told, whisking the potion rapidly with the glass rod. A dense cloud of pungent brown gas billowed from the flask and hung in the air. The apprentices coughed and spluttered.

Katerina poured the liquid into six cups. "It's very powerful, so you only need a sip," she said. "Go on—it tastes better than it smells.

"Watch me." She took a tiny sip and smiled.

Archie held his nose and tipped the cup until a small amount of the liquid spilled into his mouth. It did taste better than it smelled—but not much. The flavor reminded him of burned vinegar.

The others sipped from their cups. For a moment nothing happened, and then Archie felt a strange disruption in the air around him. He tried to move, but he felt as if the air was as thick as treacle. He heard Thistle calling him, but the words came out distorted, as if he was a toy that needed new batteries.

"Archieeeeeee. It'sssssss theeeeee potionnnnn."

Archie turned his head. Katerina was saying something now.

"Anddddd soooooooo aaaassss yoooou cannnnn seeeeeee, theeee sloooowwwww pooootiooooon issssss woooorkkiiiiing!"

Her lips drew back in a very slow smile.

"Nowwww drink theeee quickennnniiiinnng potiooooon!"

Moving at glacial speed, the apprentices drank some of the quickening potion. Archie felt the air around him speeding up. When Katerina spoke, her voice still sounded slow, but it was almost back to normal.

"Take another sip of the quickennning potiooon," she urged.

She took another sip. "That's better," she declared, sounding like her old self again. The others did the same.

"Good," said Katerina, smiling. "All back to normal now! Well, I hope that was helpful. Now if we could just find the formula for Azoth . . ."

"Believe me, we've looked," said Thistle. "We went through all the books, but there's no sign of the formula."

Katerina was staring at something on the other side of the room.

"Wait a second. What's this?" She walked across and plucked a notebook from a shelf. "Grey's notebook!" she exclaimed, beginning to riffle through it. "This is it. We've found it!"

Archie glanced at Thistle. They'd looked through the pile of papers. How could they have missed the notebook? Katerina interruped his thoughts. She started to pull jars from the shelves, frantically reading their labels as she searched for the ingredients she needed to make Azoth.

She picked up a test tube with a liquid in it. "Rain from on high," she muttered. "And the salt of the earth. The breath of life."

She examined the leather bellows and checked the notebook. "Yes, it's all here," she said. "All the ingredients have been sitting here on the shelves all these years.

"What's missing?" She consulted the notebook again. "Next we need some embers from the Flame of Pharos."

"That can be arranged," said Archie. "I'll be right back."

He returned a little while later holding some glowing embers in Old Zeb's protective glove, and placed them in a glass bowl on the bench.

"There," he said.

"Brilliant," cried Katerina. "But where's the last ingredient?" she asked, her voice rising in frustration.

She rummaged among the jars on the shelves, her face creased in concentration. "Here it is," she cried, lifting down a flask containing a small quantity of a golden dust. "Last but by no means least, the essence of magic!

"Quick, bring the flames," she urged. Soon the five flaming braziers had been placed in a circle. Katerina opened her bag and took out a crystal chalice.

"Stand behind the flames," she instructed them. The

five children took up positions, facing one another. Katerina placed one of the ingredients in front of each of them.

"Now we are ready to begin," she said, and began to read out the instructions from the notebook.

The scene resembled the one Archie had witnessed in Pudding Lane. He felt a slight migiving. Things were moving a bit too fast for his liking. He didn't want to repeat the same mistake that Grey and the other alchemists had made. Katerina caught his eye.

"Are you all right with this, Archie?" she asked. "I don't mean to take over."

Archie smiled. "You're the expert," he said. "Go for it."

Katerina smiled. "Right, then. Onward and upward. Azoth is made of the four elements: water, earth, air, and fire," she said. "Each of you must add your ingredient in the correct order, starting with you, Bramble."

She passed the chalice to Bramble, who read the label on the glass jar in front of her. "Rain from the highest mountain in the Himalayas," she said, emptying the last few drops into the crystal chalice.

"Excellent," said Katerina. "Now you, Rupert."

"Soil from the crater of a volcano," he said, sprinkling the last granules of the dust-dry powder into the water.

Arabella was next. She held up the tiny leather bellows

and put its nozzle into the glass. "The breath from a new-born babe," she said as she squeezed the last gasp from the bellows, sending bubbles of air to mingle with the other ingredients.

"And now you, Thistle."

Thistle added some glowing embers. "A light from the Flame of Pharos," he said, emptying the glowing cinders into the mixture.

"And finally," said Katerina, "the secret ingredient, the essence of magic itself. Archie?"

Archie sprinkled in the last of the golden powder. The flame went red.

"Now read the spell," urged Katerina.

Archie read out the words in the notebook:

> *"Powers of the universe*
> *Drawn by Nature's right*
> *The moment of Creation*
> *All of magic's might."*

The solution began to boil. There was a roaring noise like a flame rushing up a chimney and a blinding flash. The solution inside the flask glowed golden.

"We've done it!" cried Katerina. "We've made Azoth!"

That night as they walked home, the children were feeling very pleased with themselves. By using up all the ingredients, they had managed to make a flask of Azoth. Katerina had taken a small amount for her research, along with the notebook to see if it contained any other useful information. What remained of the Azoth was in a crystal inkwell hidden in the laboratory.

"That was brilliant!" said Bramble, still buzzing from the excitement.

"*You* were brilliant with the slow potion," said Archie admiringly. "The rest of us weren't so great."

Bramble looked pleased. "Beginner's luck," she said, grinning. "But I don't think we could have made the Azoth without Katerina."

"All we need now," said Archie, "is an enchanted quill. And we know where there are some of those. In the Scriptorium!"

CHAPTER 14

The Dark Quill

When they arrived for their next session with Gloom a few days later, Katerina was waiting at the door to the Scriptorium.

"Professor Gloom," she said, flashing her big eyes at him, "may I sit in on your assessment? I have recently discovered some interesting papers in the Archive that may be of help." She winked at the children. "I think they may shed some light on how Grey was able to write magic."

Gloom didn't seem his usual upbeat self. Archie wondered what was on his mind. He seemed distracted. "Erm, yes," he said. "Why not? We have to find a way to speed up our work."

The others had picked up on it, too. The five of them exchanged looks. They wondered what had happened that made the assessments suddenly so urgent.

When they had taken their places, Gloom smiled. "Today, I will be assessing your ability to write spells.

"The first step toward writing magic is creating spells. When those spells are written with Azoth, they will become master spells. But we don't want any . . . accidents. Forewarned is forearmed and all that. So today we will be practicing with disappearing ink."

On the desk he placed three crystal inkwells with golden lids. "The ink will last only until it dries. Then it will vanish, leaving no trace."

He coughed nervously. "This means that any spells you write today will last only a few seconds. So you can't do any permanent harm if something goes wrong!"

"Do you think he knows something we don't?" muttered Arabella under her breath.

"There's definitely something going on," whispered Bramble. "It must have to do with the curse."

"Today we will be using the enchanted quills," announced Gloom.

The children made eye contact again.

Gloom crossed to the glass cabinet and unlocked the door. He took out a long, thin box made from polished wood, with the symbol of the Golden Circle inlaid in mother-of-pearl.

"These quills belonged to the Alchemists' Club," he said. "Miraculously, those of Braxton Foxe, Angelica Ripley, and Roderick Trevallen were rescued from the burning bakery in Pudding Lane. Sadly, Fabian Grey's golden Bennu quill and that of Felicia Nightshade were not so fortunate."

He opened the lid and peered in. A puzzled look passed across his face. "I'm mistaken, there are four. . . . That must be Felicia Nightshade's black raven quill. I thought it was destroyed in the fire, but here it is."

He smiled. "So there are four quills. You will have to take turns. Thistle, you may choose first."

He held out the box. Thistle put in his hand and pulled out a white quill.

"Ah," said Gloom. "Excellent. That belonged to Angelica Ripley. It's from a Caladrius bird—which has healing powers."

Bramble went next. She held up a mottled brown quill.

"Now, that belonged to Braxton Foxe," said Gloom. "It's from a griffin, one of the great guardians of magical treasures!

"A roc feather for you, Rupert," Gloom added, as

Rupert produced a long, dark feather. "That was Roderick Trevallen's quill. And finally, Felicia Nightshade's raven quill."

"May I try that one?" asked Katerina, reaching for the black quill.

"Yes, why not?" said Gloom. "Although unless you have the Golden Circle, I fear you are wasting your time.

"We prepared three inkwells, thinking there were only three quills," he continued, "so you'll have to share with Rupert. Now, let us make a start. On your desks each of you will find a piece of parchment. I want you to imagine something from nature and try to channel your imagination into a spell. Then I want you to write down the spell. This is not easy, so you'll need to concentrate."

Bramble, Thistle, Rupert, and Katerina dipped their quills in the inkwells. There was a pause while they all tried to imagine something from nature, and then the sound of quill nibs scratching on parchment filled the air. Rupert, Bramble, and Thistle were all intent on trying to create a spell. Katerina, too, was writing frantically.

At first, nothing happened, and then Archie looked up to see a tiny blue butterfly fluttering above Rupert's head.

"That's amazing!" he cried.

"What is?" asked Rupert, who was focusing all his attention on the parchment in front of him.

"There!" cried Thistle, pointing at the butterfly.

Rupert stopped scribbling to look, and the moment he did, the ink disappeared on the parchment and the butterfly vanished.

"Oh, it's gone now!" sighed Thistle. "But it was brilliant while it lasted."

"Well done," cried Gloom, clapping his hands together excitedly. "A butterfly spell! Such a talented bunch!"

Just then, Rupert exclaimed, "Look, everyone, Bramble's writing magic!"

And she was. She had her head bowed and was totally absorbed in composing a spell. As she scratched on the parchment, a bumblebee buzzed around in the air above, flying in lazy circles around her quill.

When she saw the others looking at her, she glanced up. Again the spell vanished as soon as the ink faded.

"Well done, Bramble!" said Gloom. "Oh, and that's rather splendid too, Thistle!" he added as Thistle produced a furry brown caterpillar that crawled across his desk and then vanished.

Bramble passed her quill to Archie. "Your turn, Arch."

Archie grasped it firmly. The quill felt wonderfully balanced, with the gold nib weighting it perfectly in his hand. He reached across and dipped his quill in the inkwell on Katerina's desk.

"How are you getting on, Katerina?" asked Gloom.

Katerina was scribbling frantically. "Nothing yet," she said, a note of irritation in her voice.

"Well, what did you expect?" said Gloom. "Only those with the Golden Circle Firemark can write magic."

"It's probably the quill," said Arabella. "It looks like it's been mended at some point."

Katerina inspected the quill. "Arabella's right," she said. "It has been repaired. But that's not unusual. Magic writers get very attached to their quills and go to great lengths to make them last. Fabian Grey was so protective of his quill that he cast it in gold."

Archie took a closer look. He could see where the quill had been repaired. If it was the one Felicia had used in Pudding Lane, then it was Fabian Grey who had tried to break it. The last spell the quill had written was a curse. Archie desperately racked his brain for some way of warning Gloom without revealing how he knew.

"Erm, Professor Gloom, I think that quill is damaged," he said. "I don't think we should use it. It could be dangerous."

"What?" said Gloom. "Well, I can see that it has been well used. But I'm sure it's absolutely fine. Katerina, what do you think?"

"Yes, but the black quill is—" Archie started to say.

"Special?" interjected Katerina. "So why won't it let me write magic!"

"Never mind, Katerina," said Arabella. "Would you like me to try to write a spell for you?"

"Thank you," said Katerina, passing the black quill to Arabella. "Here," she added, handing her the inkwell.

As Arabella took it, the griffin quill in Archie's hand pulsed. He felt it fluttering in his hand like a tiny bird. Then it pulled his hand toward the parchment on his desk. As he watched, amazed, words began to appear.

For the sake of a choice
Between dark and light
The city she burned
All through the night.

Heed thou this caution
The Alchemists' Curse
Friend turn on friend
If it be not reversed.

Archie stared at the words. Where had they come from?

He was still gazing at the parchment when he heard someone scream. Arabella was clutching the raven quill with a strange look on her face. Her body had gone limp like a puppet except for the hand that held the quill, which was scribbling madly as if it had a life of its own.

Fiery black letters began to form in the air above Arabella's head.

In dark places where none may go
Shadows linger from long ago
Secrets lurk from older days
Hidden paths and stealthy ways.

"Whatever is the matter with you?" cried Gloom. "Good heavens," he added, catching sight of the black letters. "Dark magic!" He tried to snatch the quill from Arabella, but as he did, his body went rigid and the quill continued to scribble.

Where shadows hide let darkness reign
The Alchemists' Curse shall come again . . .

Gloom began to tremble violently. The other apprentices stared in horror, powerless to do anything.

And in that moment Archie heard the gentle voice he had heard before, but this time its tone was urgent.

"Do something, book whisperer! The quill is bewitched. The magic assessor needs your help! Without it he will die!"

"But I don't know how to help him!" cried Archie desperately.

"Use your gift," said the voice.

And then Archie heard another voice. It was thin and high, and at first it wavered, but then it grew stronger.

"Quill of darkness, spell of black,
By the light of Pharos, I cast you back!"

With a shock Archie realized it was his own voice. But the sound was not coming from his lips; it was coming from the parchment in front of him. His hand was moving and he was writing the words.

As he wrote, green fiery letters appeared above his head.

The black letters hanging in the air over Gloom remained a second longer and then vanished. Gloom fell forward and collapsed on the ground.

"Quickly," cried Katerina, "do something!"

"I'll get Gideon Hawke," cried Rupert. "He'll know what to do."

When Hawke arrived with Wolfus Bone and Morag Pandrama, they found Gloom on the floor surrounded by the apprentices, with frightened looks on their faces. The magic assessor was ashen, with deep shadows under his eyes.

Morag Pandrama leaned over him. "Orpheus, drink this," she said, offering him a healing potion in a cup. She poured the liquid onto Gloom's tongue, and he swallowed. His eyes flickered and then opened.

"What happened?" he asked.

"From what Rupert has told me, it sounds like you interrupted a dark spell while it was being written," Hawke said. He bent down to retrieve the black quill from the floor.

"Where did you get this quill?" he asked, passing it to Bone.

"It was in the cabinet with the others," said Gloom. "Why?"

"Because it is bewitched," said Bone, holding the quill carefully between his thumb and forefinger. "It has a hex on it. You're lucky you didn't hold it for any longer than you did. Another few seconds and you would have been dead," he added, shaking his head.

He held up the quill. "What do you want to do with it?" he asked Hawke.

"Take it to my study. We'll examine it there," said Hawke. He paused. "In fact, take all the quills to my office. They'll be safer there. No one will be tempted to use them."

The children cast desperate glances at one another. With the quills under lock and key, what chance did they have of writing any magic?

"The excitement is over," Hawke said. "You may all go back to your apprenticeships."

They began to file out. Archie was about to join them, but Hawke caught his arm. "The dark spell is trying to find a way back into the world," Hawke said. "It would have killed Gloom if you hadn't intervened. How did you break its hold on him?"

"I don't know," said Archie. "I started writing, and the words just sort of came to me."

Hawke noticed the parchment on the desk, with the spell still written on it. He picked it up and examined it.

"Did you write this?" he asked.

Archie nodded. He didn't understand why the ink hadn't disappeared.

"What ink did you use?"

"Gloom said it was disappearing ink," said Archie.

"Which inkwell did you dip your quill in?"

"That one," said Archie.

Hawke picked up the inkwell and sniffed it. Then he held it up to the light. It gleamed with gold.

"Azoth," he said. "That's why the spell didn't disappear. Was the black quill dipped in this inkwell, too?"

Archie tried to think. "Yes, I think it was."

Hawke looked thoughtful. "I think I'd better take this," he said. "In the wrong hands it could be dangerous.

"One more thing. I'd like to see Fabian Grey's ring. Do you have it?"

"It's in my bag," said Archie.

"I think we'll keep it in Lost Books for now," said Hawke. "Just until Wolfus has had a chance to examine it."

Hawke took the ring. Archie noticed that he folded the piece of parchment and put that in his pocket, too.

———

For the next few days, everyone was talking about the incident with the dark quill. There were all sorts of rumors flying around. Some were even speculating that the quill had come from the raven that had brought the ring. The elders had launched a full investigation into how the hexed quill had ended up in the cabinet with the other enchanted quills, but no one had come forward. Archie felt guilty. He had known that the black quill could be dangerous but had not tried hard enough to stop Arabella or Gloom from using it.

It was two days later when Gideon Hawke summoned Archie to his study. Hawke was sitting behind his desk. Pandrama and Bone had chairs by the fire.

"I want to talk to you about the spell you wrote the other day," said Hawke when Archie was settled on the battered leather sofa. "Simple spells are not easy, but they are nothing compared to complex magic, like charms and enchantments. That's what the old magic writers were really good at.

"They wrote in Azoth, which is why their magic has endured for so long. And the reason their spells were so strong is because they were original. No one had written them before. They are the master spells. But what you did the other day, that was an original spell."

"How do you know?" asked Archie, alarmed.

"Because Morag checked it against the texts, and she can find no record of such a spell. That means it is original to you. More than that, it's a very special sort of magic. It had to be to release Orpheus from the curse. So let's see what you can do."

He opened a drawer and took something out. Archie recognized Braxton Foxe's mottled quill. Hawke slid it across the desk to him. Then he passed him some ink and a piece of parchment. Archie picked up the quill and dipped it in the ink.

Hawke studied him. "Close your eyes and open your

imagination. Think of something from nature that is magical and picture it in your mind. When you can see it clearly, I want you to imagine it here in this room. It can be whatever pops into your head. This is about creating your own magic."

Archie closed his eyes and tried to concentrate. But nothing came to him.

"What are you thinking of, Archie?" Hawke asked after a while.

Archie's mind had gone blank. All he could picture in his mind was darkness. And then he saw something else. It was just out of sight at first, but gradually he became aware of a light.

"What can you see?" asked Hawke.

"The Flame of Pharos," said Archie. For a brief moment he felt the magic flowing through him. He felt light-headed.

"Look!" he heard Pandrama gasp. "The boy is writing magic!"

Green flaming letters had appeared in the air above Archie's head. But in the instant he became aware of them, the image of the Flame disappeared and the words vanished.

Archie felt deflated. He had been so close to creating

an original spell. He sensed the disappointment among the three elders.

"Never mind," said Hawke. "You are very young to write magic. Even Fabian Grey couldn't do it at your age." He smiled kindly.

As he was leaving, Hawke put Grey's ring in Archie's hand. "I had Wolfus examine it," he said. "There are no traces of dark magic, so you can have it back.

"Look after it," he said as Archie put it in his pocket. "And Archie, one last thing. Dark spells are always looking for a way into the world. You must be very careful that you don't allow them in through you."

CHAPTER 15

Agatha's Emporium

Christmas was approaching fast. It would be Archie's first in Oxford. He was sitting at the kitchen table in Houndstooth Road with his two cousins, sharing a plate of Loretta's mince pies. Or as Thistle called them, wince pies, because they were so bad they made you wince. Thistle had *Magical Places to Visit* propped up in front of him.

"I've been thinking," said Archie, as he watched Bramble take a big bite from a bulging mince pie and immediately pull a face, "about Fabian Grey's ring. We need to know more about it. There must be a reason the raven gave it to me."

Thistle looked up from reading his book. "Well, I think I know just the place. Listen to this," he said.

"AGATHA'S EMPORIUM OF MAGICAL MEMORABILIA is a shop in Oxford market, specializing in scrying instruments and other magical memorabilia. Agatha's caters to the more discerning magical shopper."

"That was the name of the woman selling astroscopes at the book fayre," said Bramble. "She said to ask for her at the shop."

"Well," said Archie, "she recognized the Emerald Eye, so it's worth a try."

⌒

It was frosty the next day when the three children set off for Agatha's. They made their way into the center of Oxford and into the covered market just off the high street. They wandered through the maze of little lanes. They walked all the way through a couple of times but could not see any shops that looked remotely magical. Thistle hadn't brought his compass, because they thought the Emporium would be easy to find.

"Perhaps Agatha's moved," said Thistle, his breath

like mist in the wintry air.

"No, I'm sure it's here somewhere," said Archie. "We're just not looking in the right place. Does *Magical Places to Visit* give any directions?"

Thistle consulted the book. "To find Agatha's Emporium . . . just follow your nose," he said. "That's not very helpful."

"Or maybe it is," said Archie, stopping in his tracks. "We could be looking with the wrong sense."

He took a big sniff. "I can smell something," he said.

"That'll be the fishmonger's shop," said Thistle, grinning.

"Not that," said Archie. "A sweet smell."

"Okay, now I can smell it, too," said Thistle. "Vanilla, with a hint of sulfur, and let me see—a dash of decay."

It was the smell of amora—the scent of magic. They walked through the market again, pausing occasionally to close their eyes and take a good sniff. They loitered by a greengrocer's stall for a while. The smell of fresh fruit and cut flowers smelled like Natural Magic, but then Bramble picked up a whiff of brimstone, the unmistakable scent of Mortal Magic.

"It's coming from that shop over there," she said, "past

the shoe shop, the one that's in shadow."

A small shop was tucked away in a dark corner of the market. As the three children approached, the smell of magic got stronger. The shop had red curtains across the windows and a sign that said AGATHA'S EMPORIUM: PUTTING THE MAGIC BACK INTO SHOPPING.

They opened the door and went inside. The shop was small and cluttered. A selection of magical instruments and objects had been laid out in glass cases.

Agatha stepped out into the front of the shop, wearing the same green smock as she'd had on at the fayre.

"Hello, my dears. What can I do for you? Interested in a gift for a friend or family member?"

"We met you at the book fayre," said Archie. "You were interested in my pendant."

Agatha peered at them through watery eyes. "Ah, yes. I remember you now," she said. "John Dee's scrying stone, the Emerald Eye. Have you changed your mind about selling it?"

"No," said Archie. "I'm here about something else. A ring."

"Show me, and I'll tell you what I know."

Archie hesitated. He didn't know whether he could trust Agatha. But he was desperate to find out more about the ring. He took it from his pocket and placed it on the counter.

Agatha regarded it keenly. Her bony fingers closed around it like claws and her eyes gleamed.

Archie felt Bramble and Thistle at his side, watching carefully. The little woman was making cooing noises.

"Well, well. Fabian Grey's ring," she said, sighing. "Aren't you full of surprises? Next you'll be telling me you've got his quill!" she added, watching their faces. "Where did you get the ring? Don't tell me—it was a present, too?"

Archie smiled. "Sort of," he said. He couldn't really tell her that a raven had delivered it. "What do you know about it?"

Agatha shook her head thoughtfully, a smile playing at the corners of her lips. "Fabian Grey was the greatest alchemist in England. Most people know him for the Great Fire of London, but he was also a brilliant artist and inventor. He made the ring himself."

She peered at the gold band. "There aren't many pieces that were forged in the magic flames—but I can tell that this one was."

She held it up to her eye.

"What's that?" she said, turning the ring between her

finger and thumb. "There's something written inside."

She picked up an Imagining Glass and peered through it. "The writing is very small, but I think you can just about make it out." She offered Archie the Imagining Glass and turned the ring in her hand so he could see the tiny lettering.

This is my word, this is my mark
Forged in the fire, a light in the dark.

"It must be very special to have an inscription like that. You should be careful," said Agatha. "There are some who'd give anything to get their hands on this."

"Greaders, you mean?" said Thistle.

"Collectors," Agatha said. The conversation was starting to make Archie uncomfortable. He just wanted to get the ring back, but Agatha clutched it tightly in her hand.

"How much did you say you want for it?" she asked.

"It's not for sale," Archie said.

He held out his hand for the ring, but Agatha seemed reluctant to give it back. He thought he heard something cry out, and a black bird fluttered against the shop window. Archie felt the palm of his hand start to itch.

He clasped Agatha's hand in his. He gently plucked the ring from her hand. As he tucked it back into his pocket, Agatha gave a small gasp, and her hand made a clutching movement in the air.

CHAPTER 16

Winging It

The next incident occurred a week later. Old Zeb had sent Archie to collect yeti hair and werewolf claw needles from the Mythical Menagerie. On the way, he had run into Bramble and Thistle, who were in the Natural Magic Department and decided to go with him.

As they approached the menagerie, they could hear a cacophony of screeching, flapping, and growling. When they reached the passageway between the pens, they could see that the food buckets had been knocked over. There was no sign of Rupert.

They glanced over the low gate to the snufflings' pen, but it appeared to be empty. Either the small creatures had made themselves invisible or they had escaped.

In the next pen, Desmond the dodo was flapping his pathetically short wings and honking madly. In the pen with the blacked-out glass, they could hear the man-eating birds, the Stymphalians, crashing against the wire mesh and making blood-chilling screeching sounds.

"I have a bad feeling about this," said Bramble. "Where's Rupert?"

"Look at the dryads," cried Thistle. The tree nymphs were clinging to the tops of their trees and shrieking in their high-pitched voices as loudly as they could. They were shaking their branches and pointing at something.

"I think they're trying to tell us something," said Archie. "What are they pointing at?"

Someone had placed a silver locket on top of the wall of one of the animal pens.

"It looks like Rupert's new Keep Safe. He's only had it a few days."

The locket was open. The dryads were pointing at it and covering their ears with their tiny hands.

"It must be a musical locket," said Archie. "It's too high a frequency for us to hear it, but the creatures hate it. It's driving them mad. Look!"

The golden hinds and satyrs were racing up and down

their pen, bucking and snorting. And Simon the salamander had turned an angry red. The children took cover as the salamander blasted the metal door with its flame.

Before they could close the locket, they heard the bellowing sound.

"Uh-oh," cried Bramble, pointing at where the reinforced gate to the next pen was standing open. "Someone's let the Minotaur out!"

The bellowing wasn't coming from the reinforced pen. It was coming from the large pen that held the Pegasus. They heard a frightened whinny and raced over.

The winged horse was backed into a corner, her nostrils flaring and her eyes wide with terror. Staring angrily at her through bloodshot eyes was the Minotaur, his two very sharp horns aimed menacingly at the Pegasus's exposed flank. The bull-headed monster was preparing to charge.

At that moment they spotted something else lying on the ground between the terrified winged horse and the angry Minotaur. It was Rupert—and he wasn't moving.

Bramble's hand flew to her mouth. "Rupert!" she cried, but he could not hear her. "He's hurt. He must have tried to protect the Pegasus!"

The Minotaur snorted loudly and pawed the ground

with his foot. He threw back his huge head and roared.

"Rupert'll be killed," cried Thistle, "unless we can stop the Minotaur." There was no time to reach the gate, which was standing open some twenty yards away. Thistle started to climb the fence, but Archie was already at the top. He dropped down into the pen and ran toward Rupert.

"Hey, wait for me!" cried Bramble, scrambling up the fence behind them. By now Thistle was on the other side and racing after Archie. Bramble swung her leg over the top of the fence and dropped down on the other side too. Now there were three of them running toward the confused Minotaur.

Thistle started shouting and waving his hands. The creature looked from one to the other, unsure which one of these irritating humans annoyed him most. Bramble had picked up a feeding bucket and was hitting it with a stick to make even more noise.

Archie saw that the Minotaur was momentarily distracted. He darted forward. Rupert was heavy, but Archie gripped him under his arms and managed to haul him away from the snorting Minotaur toward the Pegasus. The winged horse whinnied and tossed her head frantically, watching Archie as he tried to drag Rupert to safety.

Archie felt Rupert stir and groan something. "My ribs—I think they're broken. The Minotaur trampled me. I was trying to protect her."

The winged horse flared her nostrils in fear.

"Easy, girl," soothed Archie. "I'm going to untie your wings so you can get away."

The horse inclined her head as if perhaps she understood.

"Steady, girl," said Archie, holding up his hand to calm her. He gently stroked her head. Then, letting go of Rupert for a moment, he reached up and undid the strap that bound her wings to her body. The creature unfurled them to their full span.

The movement drew the Minotaur's attention. Thistle and Bramble were still shouting and waving their arms, but the beast's bloodshot eyes had locked on Archie and the Pegasus. He bellowed once. Then he put his head down and charged.

"Run, Archie," cried Bramble, desperately reaching for the tiny gold bow-and-arrow charm on her Keep Safe. But there wasn't time for her to take aim at the charging Minotaur.

Archie was cornered. There was only one thing he could do. Hauling Rupert to his feet, he shoved him over the Pegasus's back and scrambled up after him.

For a moment, the great winged horse stared wide-eyed as the Minotaur bore down on her. Then, when the beast was almost upon her, when Archie had almost given up hope, the creature beat her powerful wings and launched herself into the air. She soared upward, and Archie held on to her long white mane with one hand and on to Rupert with the other.

Thistle and Bramble cheered as the flying horse swooped around the pen. The Minotaur, unable to slow his charge, crashed into the fence, roaring with anger. For a moment he was dazed, but then he shook his head and began to paw the ground again.

"Erm, Bram," said Thistle, "I think it's time to go!"

"I'm with you," cried Bramble. "Run!"

They sprinted for the gate. Behind them they could hear the Minotaur's hooves tearing up the ground and getting closer and closer. Bramble reached the gate first and darted through it. Thistle was a fraction behind her, and the Minotaur a fraction behind him. But it was just enough time for Bramble to let Thistle through and then slam the gate shut. With a loud thump and a sound of splintering wood, the Minotaur smashed into the gate, knocking himself senseless.

Bramble dusted herself down. She marched over to the silver locket and closed it. The magical creatures immediately began to calm down.

Bramble gave a low whistle. "Phew. That was close," she breathed. "Where are Archie and Rupert?"

"Over there," cried Bramble, pointing. "I think they're enjoying themselves. Look!"

She was right—the Pegasus was soaring over the animal pens, her long mane and tail streaking out behind her. Rupert was now sitting astride the beautiful creature behind Archie, holding on around her middle with one hand and clutching his ribs with the other.

~

Inside the Lost Books Department half an hour later, Gideon Hawke paced back and forth, his brow furrowed. Feodora Graves and Orpheus Gloom were sitting in armchairs on either side of the fire, watching him. Archie and Rupert sat on the gnarled leather sofa in the middle of the room.

Rupert was trying to explain what had happened.

"One minute it was fine," he said. "The next thing I remember is opening the locket, and then all hell broke loose."

"Well, someone knew you'd take it into the menagerie,"

said Graves, holding up the musical locket. "In fact, they were relying on it. This is a very nasty little piece of work."

"It looks harmless enough, but it has a hex on it," said Hawke. "The tune it plays bewitches the person who opens it and drives magical creatures mad."

"Where did you get it?" asked Gloom.

"Well, that's the odd thing about it—I thought it was from you!" said Rupert. "It came with a letter saying that the five apprentices with the Golden Circle Firemark must all have Keep Safes, and the locket was mine." He paused. "So it wasn't from you?"

"Certainly not!" said Gloom.

"Well, who was it from, then?"

"I wonder," said Hawke. "Did anyone else receive a Keep Safe?"

Rupert thought for a moment. "Archie got the ring from the raven," he said.

"Hmmm, yes, the ring," said Hawke thoughtfully. "But this," he added, indicating the musical locket, "is a different matter altogether. And it just arrived out of the blue?"

"I lost my lucky cuff links and it arrived shortly afterward, gift wrapped and everything."

"Some gift. If it hadn't been for Archie's quick

thinking—it would have been fatal for you," said Hawke.

Archie smiled. Tucked inside his shirt was a single white feather.

"The Pegasus was grateful, too," he said.

"I'll second that!" said Rupert. "I owe you one, Arch."

Graves's expression was serious. "First the accident with the dark quill, and now this," she said, shaking her head.

"They were no accidents, Feodora," said Hawke, his brow darkening. "The Alchemists' Curse has returned."

CHAPTER 17

The Foul-Weather Friend

The second half of December brought frosty weather and a few flurries of snow to Oxford. The children were disappointed it didn't settle. The work of the museum carried on all year, but apprenticeships were suspended for the Christmas holidays.

Under normal circumstances, the children would have been happy to pass the time talking about the presents they were hoping to get. But there was a shadow hanging over the members of the Alchemists' Club. The incident with Rupert and the hexed Keep Safe was weighing on all their minds.

Whoever had sent Rupert the locket was still at large,

despite attempts by the elders to discover who was responsible.

Nor had they managed to find out any more about the Alchemists' Curse. It seemed to be the museum's best-kept secret.

———

The first morning of the holiday break, Loretta called up the stairs.

"Archie, something came for you in the mail. It's on the kitchen table."

Archie felt his spirits lift. He guessed it was from Gran, who was still on her road trip. Sure enough, a padded white envelope was addressed to him in her neat handwriting.

Inside was a brightly wrapped gift, with a card that read: *To Archie, Bramble, and Thistle. Merry Christmas. Love from Granny Greene. P.S. Don't open until Christmas Day.*

With the parcel was a letter addressed to Archie. Hungry for news, he tore it open and started to read.

Dearest Archie,

I'm sorry I can't be there with you at this special time of year, but I am thinking about the three of you.

The reason I am writing to you separately is to tell you what I have discovered on my travels.

As you know, before he left, your father made me promise to keep you away from magic for as long as possible. If that failed, I was to find out as much as I could about Fabian Grey. It is known among certain magical aides that your fate and his are linked in some way.

What I tell you here is what I have been able to piece together. Grey escaped the blaze in the baker's shop and returned to Oxford, where he was arrested and taken to the Tower of London.

It seems that he was badly affected by what happened in the cellar and lost his memory from the shock. Somehow even in his poor state of mind he managed to escape and left England. I have traced his movements to the Himalayas. Where he went from there, I do not yet know.

There are questions that need answers, and I cannot return until I find them. Keep your cousins close by, and share this letter with them if you want to.

Give my love to them and to Loretta and Woodbine.

Merry Christmas.

All my love as ever,
Gran

Archie showed the letter to his cousins.

"The raven that brought the ring said it came from the tower," said Bramble thoughtfully. "And the Tower of London is famous for its ravens, so that might explain it. But why didn't Grey leave the country straightaway? Why risk traveling to Oxford? It's the first place the authorities would have looked for him."

"Maybe he'd already lost his memory by then, or was confused?" said Thistle.

"He had enough wits to find his way back here," said Archie. "There must have been something he needed to do. Some unfinished business."

Just then, they heard Loretta calling them from downstairs.

"It'll have to wait," said Thistle. "Mum wants us to help decorate the tree."

The Christmas preparations were a welcome distraction from their worries. The children hung magic lanterns from the ceiling and cut out Christmas trees from scraps of parchment that Archie had rescued from the workshop. They festooned the tree with tinsel and other decorations and put the gifts underneath, with the package from Gran in pride of place.

Arabella dropped by with some good news. Rupert was on the mend and seemed to have suffered no long-term effects from the Minotaur attack.

"He's still very pale," said Arabella, who looked ashen herself. "He's cracked a couple of ribs, but they don't think there's any lasting damage."

"Well, thank heavens for that," said Bramble.

"What kind of nutter sends someone a hexed Keep Safe?" said Thistle. "I mean, you'd have to be pretty sick."

"Yes," agreed Arabella, looking upset again. "He could have been seriously hurt."

The Foxe family celebrated Christmas Eve with their usual gusto. Woodbine and Loretta drank hot mulled wine and sang a raucous rendition of the thirteen days of Christmas (the one with "six magicians spelling" and "a phoenix in a fig tree"). The children hung up their stockings.

Christmas Day was clear and sunny, and the children raced downstairs to open their presents. Archie received three pairs of socks and a new dressing gown. Thistle got the same. Bramble got socks and a new woolen hat with a pom-pom. Most intriguing of all was the joint present to the three of them from Granny Greene.

Inside was an instrument that looked like a clock, with a circular face and two hands that pointed to two dials. Written on the smaller dial was a list of weather conditions: Dry, Drizzle, Rain, Sleet, Mist, Fog, Hailstones, Gale, Storm, and Snow. The outside of the larger dial indicated the severity of the weather, ranging from Normal to Bad, to Worse, to Awful, to Dreadful, to Dire, to Appalling, to Frightful, to Shockingly Bad, to Absolutely Atrocious.

At the moment the short hand was pointing to Dry, and the longer hand was pointing at Normal. In a small window on one side of the face a picture of a smiling sunbeam was showing.

A note with it said:

To Archie, Bramble, & Thistle. Your very own Foul-Weather Friend! Use it wisely. Merry Christmas,
Love, Gran.

"It's a local weather generator," said Woodbine when they asked him. "It can control the weather in the area immediately around it. You move the hands to set the weather you want."

"Brilliant!" said Thistle, who loved magical instruments. "What sort of range does it have?"

"About as far as the end of the garden," said Woodbine.

"I can't wait to try it out!" said Thistle.

"Just be careful," said Woodbine. "You're not meant to use it outside of magical premises. And don't use it at home—it'll make the neighbors suspicious."

Loretta cooked Christmas lunch with all the trimmings. There were all the usual ingredients but in unusual combinations. So the turkey was served with brandy butter and trifle, followed by a generous serving of Christmas pudding with brussels sprouts. Archie reasoned that it was all going to the same place anyway and wolfed it down with barely a second thought. It was just as well, because otherwise, with the speed with which the Foxes ate, he might have missed out.

———

The five members of the Alchemists' Club had agreed to meet at the lab on Boxing Day to discuss progress. They hadn't seen one another for a few days, so they were excited to catch up. The bookshop was closed over Christmas, but Archie let them in with his key.

It was cold inside the shop and even colder in Grey's lab. But they lit a fire and the room began to warm up. Rupert still looked a bit peaky but seemed to be almost back to his old self. "I'm feeling a lot better," he said, catching Archie's eye. "Thanks."

Thistle produced the Foul-Weather Friend and put

it on the bench, his eyes gleaming. "Check this out," he said proudly. He pushed a button on the top and the glass cover flipped open. "What shall I set it to?"

"Snow, of course!" said Archie. "The more the better."

Thistle moved the shorter hand until it pointed at Snow. Inside the tiny window, the picture still showed a smiling sun.

"How long do you think it will take to work?"

Thistle stood up. "I'll have a look outside," he said. He was gone a few minutes and then came back shaking his head.

"Nothing so far," he said. "Not even any snow clouds." He looked disappointed.

"Well, it probably takes a while," said Archie, trying to sound upbeat. "What about the other hand? Maybe that will speed things up."

"Good idea," said Thistle. He moved the longer hand from Normal to Dreadful. "That should do it," he said.

"When you two have quite finished," interrupted Arabella, "some of us would like to get down to club business."

They said the Alchemists' oath.

"We have some news on Grey," said Archie. "He came back to Oxford before he was arrested and put in the Tower of London."

They explained about the letter from Granny Greene.

Arabella looked awkward, as if she needed to get something off her chest. "I've been thinking about it over Christmas. First the black quill and then Rupert's narrow escape. This whole business has gone too far. We're out of our depth. Someone is going to get seriously hurt—or even killed."

"But it's too late to stop now," said Archie. "And even if we do, it doesn't mean the curse will go away."

"Archie's right," said Bramble. "It's not just the museum we're trying to save—it's our own skins!"

"Let's put it to a vote," said Rupert. "All those in favor of continuing, raise your hand."

Archie, Thistle, Bramble, and Rupert all raised their hands.

"Those against?"

Arabella shrugged. "It will end badly," she said. "I just know it will. I've seen what magic can do to people. It brings out the worst in them."

She looked away. "But if you are all determined to see it through, then so am I."

"Great. Now that that's all sorted," said Thistle, "I'm going to get a cake from Quill's—I'm starving!"

He disappeared up the passageway but was back

quickly, wearing a big grin. "Thought you might want to know it's snowing! You've got to see it. It's amazing! Total blizzard."

Archie glanced at the Foul-Weather Friend and saw that an icon of a snowflake had appeared in the place where the smiling sun had been before.

The children ran up the stairs and through the bookshop. Out the shopwindow they could see the air was full of dancing snowflakes as big as leaves and fluffy like cotton balls. The courtyard was white, and the stairs down to Quill's had almost disappeared under a snowdrift.

"Brilliant!" cried Archie, as they all ran back to get their gloves and hats and piled out into the fresh snowfall.

"I told you!" cried Thistle, racing out into the white courtyard, leaving a trail of footprints in the new snow. "Hey! Who threw that?" he shouted as a snowball exploded on his shoulder, showering him with fine white powder.

He turned to see Archie grinning and ready to launch another snowball in his direction. Just then Archie was showered in white powdery snow as a snowball splattered behind his head on the front door of the bookshop.

"Drat, missed!" roared Arabella, bending down to make another one.

For the next hour, they played happily in the snow. Archie, Bramble, and Arabella built a snow fort at one end of the courtyard, while Rupert and Thistle built their own near the old bookshop. Then they launched an aerial bombardment at each other. The snow fight ended with a surprise attack by Thistle, which backfired spectacularly when he was ambushed by Arabella, who put a snowball down the inside of his sweater.

"Brrrrrrr! That's cheating," cried Thistle.

"Nonsense," said Arabella. "Haven't you ever heard of a cold war?"

After that, they called a truce and worked together to build the biggest snowman they could. When it was finished, it was nearly as tall as Rupert. Bramble put her old woolen hat on it.

"He can keep it," she said. "I got a new one for Christmas."

They were just putting the finishing touches on it when they heard Pink's voice calling them from the bottom of the steps to Quill's.

She held up a large jug of steaming hot chocolate. "Thought you might like something to warm you up."

The children gratefully went inside, dripping puddles of water as the snow on their clothes melted. Pink put their wet gloves on the radiators, and they gulped down the warming chocolate.

"Haven't seen snow like this for years," said Pink, placing a plate of mince pies on the table in front of them. "Odd thing is that there was no mention of it on the weather report."

She gave them a curious look. "What are you lot looking so guilty about, anyway?"

"Nothing," said Bramble, grinning at the others and taking a big bite from a mince pie.

———

"Freak weather conditions in the center of Oxford today caught shoppers by surprise," announced the radio presenter on the news that evening. "Up to a foot of snow fell in just a few minutes this afternoon in a small area of the city, confounding the weather reports."

In the kitchen of 32 Houndstooth Road, Woodbine raised his eyebrows.

"I don't suppose you three know anything about that?" asked Loretta suspiciously.

Archie, Bramble, and Thistle all avoided her gaze.

"Well?"

"Erm," mumbled Thistle. "Sorry, Mum, but I've got some research to do."

He nudged Archie. "Me, too," Archie murmured.

"Bramble?"

"Is that the time?" muttered Bramble. "Must dash. I said I'd help Rupert muck out the animals in the menagerie."

Loretta's dark look followed them out of the kitchen.

The three cousins were glad to get out of the house and away from Loretta's quizzical gaze. The Alchemists' Club had agreed to meet that night to try out the white quill from the Pegasus. They were excited about the prospect of writing magic.

When they arrived at the bookshop, most of the snow had gone. Rupert and Arabella were already waiting outside. Arabella was holding a book.

"It was on the doorstep," she said.

"Someone must have forgotten we're closed for Christmas," said Archie as he unlocked the door and let them in. "Is there a note with it?"

"Doesn't seem to be," said Arabella.

"We'd better take it in with us."

They trooped through the bookshop and down the stairs. Archie opened the black door and let them into the lab. It was freezing; so cold they could see their breath as mist. Rupert lit the fire and Bramble found some candles, and soon the room began to feel cozy.

Archie took the Pegasus quill from his bag and laid it on the bench. He had already cut it into a nib using one of Old Zeb's sharp knives. He rubbed his hands together to try to get some blood circulating so he could hold it. Bramble retrieved the Azoth from its hiding place behind the plaque and placed it next to the quill.

"I think we're ready," said Archie when everything was in position. "Now all we need to do is imagine a spell!"

He picked up the quill and dipped it in the Azoth. The liquid magic formed a golden nib, and he felt it vibrate with energy. He closed his eyes and tried to concentrate, but his mind was blank.

A minute passed. Then another. And another. The five of them sat in silence while Archie desperately tried to create a spell. The minutes turned into half an hour, and still they sat expectantly.

Finally, Arabella broke the silence.

"Aren't you going to examine this book?" she asked.

"No," said Archie. "It could be from anyone."

"There is a note after all. I didn't see it before. It's tucked into the pages," said Arabella.

She undid the clasp.

Archie looked up sharply. "No, don't—"

But Arabella had already opened the cover.

There was a peal of laughter, and a small figure the size of a doll and dressed in a harlequin costume sprang from the book. Too late Archie realized it was a Grabber!

He dived for the quill and Azoth, but the figure was too quick. With a shriek of laughter, it snatched both and dived back inside the book. With a final howl of laughter and a puff of smoke, the book vanished.

The children stared at one another in total bewilderment. They had just seen their best chance of rewriting *The Book of Charms* go up in smoke.

CHAPTER 18

The Asylum Seekers

January arrived with a chilly vengeance. The days were short and dark when the children resumed their apprenticeships.

In fact, the whole mood around the museum seemed chillier than usual—and not just because of the weather. The Permission Wall was getting weaker, and the elders seemed unable to do anything to stop it.

The Alchemists' Club hadn't met since the Grabber had stolen the quill and the Azoth. Even if they could have got ahold of another quill from the Pegasus, the ingredients for making more Azoth were all used up.

Their despondency increased when Woodbine returned

from another trip with more bad news. The book he had been trying to locate had disappeared. Worse was to come when rumors began circulating that the Greaders were about to get a darchemist. The final straw was the news that someone had broken into Gideon Hawke's office and stolen the black quill.

The elders summoned Archie to a meeting in Hawke's office. He didn't like being singled out from the others and wondered what it was about. With a sense of foreboding, he climbed the marble staircase to the Lost Books Department.

The discussion in Hawke's office was getting heated as Archie was ushered to a chair by Hawke's desk.

"I really don't think we have any choice but to pursue my line of inquiry," Gloom was saying. "It is clear that the museum is in great danger. We have no alternative. We must consult *The Book of Prophecy*."

"But *that book* nearly drove Fabian Grey insane," said Hawke.

"Yes, but that's where Archie comes in," said Gloom. "As I made quite clear in my assessment, he is the most magically talented of the apprentices. He has the best chance of success. He could find out what the future holds. If he used his retro-specter, he'd be quite safe."

Gloom turned to Archie. "Did you have any luck with discovering your magical name?"

"Erm, well, I meant to tell you," said Archie sheepishly. "I think I have an idea what it might be."

"Well, there you are then," said Gloom.

So that was what it was about! Gloom wanted him to consult *The Book of Prophecy*, but the elders were reluctant.

"Well, if it's the only way—" Archie started.

But before he could finish, Hawke interrupted.

"Even with a retro-specter, it is too risky."

Gloom gave Hawke a searching look. "Your concern for Archie is commendable, Gideon. But if you are so worried about sending him, perhaps you should go in his place? We all know you have magical ability. Why won't you let me assess your own talents?"

Hawke looked away.

"What are you afraid of? That Archie can do what you cannot?"

"Well, I have to agree with Orpheus," said Brown. "If Archie is willing, then we must use his talents."

Hawke looked at the ceiling. "Not yet," he said. "*The Book of Prophecy* must be our last resort."

"But we cannot simply wait for the charms to fail,"

said Graves. "The Greaders will not give up. Amos Roach is very persistent. The only good news in any of this is that Pink seems to have unjammed the Door Ray, but that won't protect the museum if the Permission Wall fails. We need to lift the curse."

"There's something I'd like to try," said Hawke, his brow furrowing. "Arthur Ripley knows more about the history of the museum than anyone alive. I propose to visit him in the asylum and ask for his help."

"Arthur Ripley is a hopeless case," snorted Wolfus Bone.

"Almost certainly," said Hawke, "but I keep in touch with the asylum to see how he is getting on. It's wise to keep tabs on him. He was the leader of the last Greader plot, after all."

"Has Arthur Ripley had any visitors?" asked Graves.

"No," said Hawke. "But he does get letters from time to time. They are all signed with the same initials—A.R."

"That will be his granddaughter, Arabella, I imagine," said Graves. "Or Roach."

Archie's ears pricked up. Could Arabella be passing information to her grandfather?

"That's what I'd thought," said Hawke. "Anyway, I plan to pay Ripley a visit."

"You can't trust him," said Bone. "He tried to kill Archie before!"

"I didn't say I was going to trust him, and I didn't say it was going to be easy," said Hawke. "But I think Ripley knows something. When he was head of Lost Books, he searched the Darchive, and I think he found something in there."

"What was it, Gideon?" asked Gloom.

"I don't know," admitted Hawke.

"He wouldn't tell you," said Bone. "He despises you."

Hawke smiled. "That is what I am relying on. He hates me so much that he will be unable to resist the urge to gloat. And the one person he might hate even more than me is Archie, which is why I plan to take him with me. If he's willing."

Graves pursed her lips. "I suppose it's worth a try. What do you say, Archie? Are you willing to face Ripley?"

Archie nodded. He didn't know how he would feel confronting the man who had tried to kill him. But he was prepared to do whatever it took to lift the curse and save the museum.

———

The next day Archie caught a train to London with Hawke. They took a bus from the station and then walked the last half mile until they stood in front of a redbrick building. There were spiky iron railings outside and bars on the windows.

The sign on the door said THE ASYLUM. RESPITE FOR THE MAGICALLY ILL. Hawke knocked three times on the door. A small hatch slid open and two eyes peered out. A voice spoke.

"Ah, Gideon, it is you."

A tall man with gray hair opened the door. "It's been a long time. How have you been? Do you need your old room?"

Archie stared at the man. He and Hawke obviously knew each other well. Hawke had never mentioned working at the asylum. Or had he been a patient? Perhaps Hawke's magical ability had unbalanced his mind? Perhaps it was a burden for all those who had magical ability.

The head of Lost Books shook his head. "No, I am well, Rumold, thank you."

"Then what, my old friend?" said Rumold.

Hawke gave a thin smile. "This is Archie Greene," he said.

"Ah, the book whisperer," said Rumold.

Archie gave him a sharp look. He didn't like it that everyone he met was so fascinated by his unusual talent. People knowing his business made Archie uncomfortable. Perhaps they expected him to end up in the asylum, too.

"We've come to see Arthur Ripley," said Hawke.

Rumold led them along a corridor to a locked room. He opened a grille in the door.

"You have visitors, Arthur."

Rumold unlocked the door. Arthur Ripley sat at a table. His face was badly scarred from the fire he had started at the museum twelve years earlier when he'd tried to steal the Terrible Tomes. His cold gray eyes glinted with malice when he saw them.

"Gideon, I wasn't expecting to see you so soon," he said. "And you brought young Archie Greene as well. How exciting! To what do I owe the pleasure?"

"I need information," said Hawke.

"Shame—I thought it was a social call," sneered Ripley. "Whatever it is you want, it must be important to drag you here." A smile flickered on his lips. "But of course I'm forgetting that you know the place well, don't you?"

Hawke looked away.

"So if you're not here on a social call, let me guess," sneered Ripley. "You are here because the magic that protects the museum is failing."

"The old magic is stronger than you realize," said Hawke. "It has lasted a thousand years, and it will outlast you. I am here because I need to know what you found in the Darchive."

It was Ripley's turn to look away. Hawke pressed him. "Surely even you do not wish to see the museum destroyed, Arthur. You were not always like this. If there is any decency left in you, help me."

Ripley gave a bitter laugh. "You disappoint me, Gideon. I thought you'd be able to work it out for yourself. After all, you are the head of Lost Books now. You have access to all those wonderful books and their secrets."

Hawke shook his head. "I have searched through all the texts, but I cannot find it—and I'm running out of time."

"Time!" groaned Ripley bitterly. "Don't talk to me about time." His eyes smoldered with anger. "You see, in here I have all the time in the world. Time to think. Time to read. Time to write letters."

Archie glanced at the book on the bedside table. He thought it had a symbol of an eye on the cover, but before he could be sure, Ripley turned it over.

Hawke was speaking again. "What do you know about the curse?"

"I know that it was put on the members of the Alchemists' Club and their descendants," said Ripley, slyly.

"But what is it?" demanded Hawke. "What does it do?"

Ripley looked amused. "I'll make a bargain with you, Gideon. If you get me out of here, I'll tell you what I know."

"I can't do that," said Hawke, "as you know full well. But I'll put in a good word."

"A good word!" snorted Ripley sarcastically. "And will you put in a good word for me, Archie? You know I never meant you any harm. If only you'd had the sense to help me release Barzak, the new age of magic would have begun by now. Such a shame you had to spoil it all."

Ripley flared into a sudden rage. "That's the trouble with the Greenes—always spoiling things. Your father was the same. If he hadn't stolen that book from me, we could have done great things together. But I couldn't trust him after that. That's why I had to . . ." He stopped. "He gave me no choice. Can't think why he wanted the book anyway. It wasn't as if it was powerful or anything."

Archie's father had been Ripley's assistant but was expelled from the museum because Ripley alleged he had stolen a book from his private collection. Archie couldn't accept that his father was a thief. He felt his anger rising.

"What do you know about my father?"

Ripley looked away. "Your father was a fool. He put himself in danger. I never intended to hurt you," he said.

"That was just a little misunderstanding. But now you need my help. Funny how it all turns around, isn't it?" he sneered.

Hawke gave a thin smile. "We will prevail, Arthur— with or without your help. I know you disturbed something in the Darchive when you opened it."

Ripley's smile vanished. He raised his hand in front of his face as if to ward off some unwanted memory. But almost immediately his expression changed from fear back to anger.

"You have no idea what lurks in the dark places of the world," he spat. "There are evils that you cannot imagine."

"What did you find?" said Hawke. "I need to know, Arthur."

For a moment, Ripley hesitated. "What Fabian Grey put there," he said, watching Hawke's face for a reaction.

"That doesn't help," said Hawke, his face a mask.

A smile twitched at the corner of Ripley's lips. "You'll find out soon enough." He turned to Archie. "The funny thing is I think your father suspected what I'd found all along—that's why he took the journal."

He looked away.

Until now Archie had had no idea which book his father had taken. Now he knew it was a journal. Ripley had given him a clue.

"Some say Grey turned into a raven," said Ripley, laughing. "Just flew away. And no one's found him yet."

What was Ripley driving at? "But he'd be over three hundred and fifty years old by now," Archie said dismissively.

Ripley's eyes flashed. "Then the curse must have passed on to his descendant. That would be you!"

"I'm a Greene, not a Grey," said Archie, but even as he said it, he felt a sudden doubt.

A knowing smile flickered across Ripley's face. "Really, Gideon, I'm disappointed in you. You've been keeping secrets. You didn't tell the boy, did you?"

"Didn't tell me what?" demanded Archie, suddenly unsure of himself.

Ripley gave him a curious look. "That you are both," he said. "Didn't you ever wonder about the color of your eyes?"

"It's Magician's Eye," said Archie. "I have one eye that is green and one that is . . ." He didn't finish the sentence.

"Yes," said Ripley, "one part Greene and one part Grey. Your father was a Greene and your mother was a Grey."

Archie stared at Ripley. He felt like he'd been punched in the stomach. He couldn't breathe.

"Didn't they tell you your mother's maiden name,

Archie? Really, how thoughtless of them. And the Greys have such a colorful history, too! But then the Grey name isn't exactly something to shout about, is it?"

Archie couldn't believe what he was hearing. It couldn't be true, could it?

He turned to Hawke to refute Ripley's claim. Hawke looked away, and Archie knew it was true. His whole world had just turned upside down.

———

Archie brooded all the way home. He was angry with Hawke for not telling him he was related to Fabian Grey. He wondered how many other people at the museum knew and had known all along. But mostly he was angry with Gran and the Foxes. Why hadn't they told him? What else were they keeping from him?

As soon as he got home, Archie confronted Loretta and Woodbine.

"You knew!" he accused them angrily.

"We should have told you before," said Loretta quietly. "But we didn't want to alarm you. Before she married your father, your mother was Amelia Grey.

"After Fabian Grey was disgraced, the Grey family name wasn't something to brag about, so she was happy to swap it for Greene when she married. But she felt responsible."

"Responsible for what?" demanded Archie.

"For you being a Grey. Your father came here one night very shaken. He said that your life was in great danger because you were descended from Fabian Grey, and he had to find somewhere safe for your mother and sister because they were also at risk."

Archie felt the hair on the back of his neck stand up. "So they didn't die in a ferry accident?"

He suddenly realized that he'd never fully believed the story Gran had told him. Some part of him had refused to accept it.

Loretta shook her head. "No," she said softly. "Mum thought it was better you thought they were dead than know what happened to them. I'm sure Alex meant to bring the family back together as soon as it was safe, but something happened and he never got the chance."

Archie felt his stomach drop. Everything he thought he knew about his family was a lie.

Loretta gave a big sigh. "You're right," she said. "It was wrong of us. But you seemed happy here and we didn't want to upset you."

"We should have told you," said Woodbine.

Archie couldn't breathe. His heart was pounding in his chest.

His family could be alive! Archie felt light-headed. A surge of hope blazed through him like a forest fire. But in the same instant he felt like he had been cheated. Cheated out of what he didn't know: the opportunity to know them, perhaps? He was overloaded with emotions.

"Your father knew that you were in danger, but he didn't know where the danger would come from," said Woodbine. "That's why he consulted *The Book of Prophecy* that night."

Loretta shook her head sadly. "I begged him not to. *The Book of Prophecy* is too powerful for mortals. All those who have ever consulted it have lost their minds."

"What did my father find out? What did the book show him?"

Loretta exchanged anxious glances with Woodbine. "We don't know, dear," she said. "After he left that night, we never saw him or your mother again."

⁓

"All these years and Mum and Dad never let on!" said Thistle, his eyes wide, when Archie told his cousins what he'd found out. Archie could see they were as shocked as he was. "I thought we knew all the family secrets."

"So you're descended from Fabian Grey," said Bramble. "Well, that explains a few things. That's why the raven gave you his ring. You seem to have inherited Grey's magical gifts. You're the book whisperer and the one with the forked fate."

She paused. "The question is, what are you supposed to do with your magical talents?"

"I'm not sure yet," said Archie. "But we need to lift the curse somehow or none of us will live long enough to find out."

━━

That night Archie lay awake. Finally he was beginning to understand why his father had wanted to keep him away from magic. It was to protect him. And it was to protect the other members of his family that Alex Greene had sent them away.

Archie's father had consulted *The Book of Prophecy*. It must have shown him that his son would be in danger from Barzak when he started his apprenticeship. But what else had it shown him that had made him think his family should go into hiding?

There was only one thing to do. Archie would have to consult *The Book of Yore* again.

CHAPTER 19

The Book of Prophecy

When Archie told his cousins what he'd decided to do, they were worried but reluctantly agreed it was their best chance of finding out what had happened to his father and lifting the curse.

"We'll be waiting right outside," said Bramble the next morning as they approached the Scriptorium. "If you're not back in one hour, we're going straight to Gideon Hawke. Is that clear?"

Archie nodded gravely. "Well, here goes," he said, his hand on the door handle. "Wish me luck."

The torches blazed as he entered the room. For a moment, he paused to study the painting again. Now that he knew he was descended from Fabian Grey, he looked to see if there was a likeness. Did Grey have magicians' eye like him? It was impossible to tell, because in the picture Grey was turning away, his face hidden.

Archie thought about the paint spilled on the floor of Grey's lab and wondered if the picture had been another of his experiments.

Gloom had said the painting contained a prophecy about the future of magic.

The Book of Yore was in its usual place. Archie approached it slowly, gripping the Emerald Eye in his hand.

"Gadabout," he said. The crystal began to pulse as it had before, and Archie felt as if he was slipping out of his own body once more. For a moment he gazed at himself, his hand still gripping the pendant. There was no time to waste.

He addressed the question to *The Book of Yore* in a clear voice. "What happened to my father?"

The book was silent. No pages ruffled.

Archie tried again. "What did my father discover in *The Book of Prophecy?*"

Silence.

The Book of Yore remained firmly shut.

"Why do you not obey me?" Archie demanded. "I command you to tell me!"

The book was still, but Archie heard something, a murmur like a breeze blowing through the brittle branches of a long-dead tree.

"The past is gone. Those who disturb it may not change it, or they may be changed by it." Archie thought he could hear more menace in the voice than usual, as if it was warning him not to cross a line.

"Yes, I know," said Archie. "But I need an answer to my question."

The book flipped open. Its pages ruffled, but when it slammed shut, there was no bookmark.

"I cannot help you, book whisperer," the voice said.

"But you contain the history of magic," cried Archie. "If you don't know, then who does?"

Silence.

Archie felt a crushing disappointment. He had been so certain that *The Book of Yore* would be able to tell him the answers.

He was about to turn away when he heard another voice.

"Some secrets are best left that way, book whisperer." It was the same gentle voice he'd heard when he'd sat at Grey's desk.

"Who are you?" he demanded.

He was gripped by a sudden fear. He took a step back.

"Are you one of the Terrible Tomes?"

"No," said the voice, "I am not one of the seven, though I wield a power more terrible than any of them, for I foretell the fate of men."

Archie spun around. The voice was coming from the glass dome where the Books of Destiny were kept.

Inside, *The Book of Charms* lay limp and silent. But that wasn't the book he was staring at.

"I know who you are," he cried, his heart beating fast. "You are *The Book of Prophecy.*"

"Yes," the voice said, "I am the guardian of destiny. *The Book of Yore* will not help you because your quest does not lie in the past. The knowledge you seek is in the future."

Archie hesitated, unsure whether to trust the voice. He had been deceived by a Terrible Tome before.

The voice sensed his unease. "I mean you no harm, book whisperer. I ask only that you listen to what I have to say. It is a story that begins in the past. But its ending is yet to be written."

Archie took a deep breath. "All right," he said.

The glass dome swung open. The voice gently continued, "I do not tell the certain future, only the possible futures.

"To know the future is a weight too heavy for most to

carry. It has driven many to madness, Fabian Grey among them. Are you ready to take that risk?"

Archie started. What was it that Grey was so desperate to discover that he risked his sanity? And Archie's father, too.

Archie's mind was racing. John Dee had warned him not to use the Emerald Eye to see his own destiny. But this was to lift the curse and save the museum. Besides, *The Book of Prophecy* had said it did not tell the future, it only prophesized about it. Archie wasn't sure what the difference was, but he hoped there was one.

"I am ready," he said.

The Book of Prophecy suddenly towered over him. Its cover had become a door with a large brass door knocker. Archie wasn't sure whether the book had grown or he had shrunk.

The door swung open, and with his heart beating fast, Archie stepped over the threshold.

He found himself in a large, poorly lit room. All around him were bookcases, forming a labyrinth. Each was jammed with old books.

"Welcome to the Library of Lives," said the voice.

Archie gazed around him at the books. He could see that there were things written on their spines. When he looked closer, he realized they were names.

"This way," said the voice. Candles lit a path to show him the way. Shadows loomed at him from unexpected angles.

The candles led him farther and farther into the labyrinth. Archie wondered if he would ever find his way out. But soon he forgot about leaving. As he passed between the bookcases, he caught glimpses of aisles that were closed off by thick cobwebs.

Ahead of him, a bookshelf blocked his path. He read the name on the spine of the first book. With a start he realized it was his own.

ARCHIBALD OBADIAH GREENE.

"The future awaits," said the voice.

Archie reached forward and took the book from the shelf. He hesitated for a moment. The voice had said he would have to trust it. Making up his mind, he opened the cover.

At first Archie could see only blank pages, but as he watched, moving images appeared. Like an old silent movie, moments from his life flashed before him.

On the day of his twelfth birthday, he saw himself answering the door to Horace Catchpole and snatching the package from his hand. The scene changed and he was catching the flame that Old Zeb had thrown for his Flame test. And now he was standing on the doorstep outside number 32 Houndstooth Road, hesitating before he knocked for his first meeting with the Foxes.

He heard the soft voice in his head. "These are the moments that shaped your destiny. They were the result of your own choices. Each led to the next and altered what followed."

The scene darkened. Archie saw himself facing Barzak and watched himself cast the spell that had banished the warlock back into *The Book of Souls*.

"This was the first fork in your fate," the voice said. "The future of magic rested on you in that moment, just as it once rested on Fabian Grey. You might have succumbed to Barzak's will, but you did not. In that instant, magic took another course. Have you seen enough, book whisperer?"

Archie shook his head. "What of the future?"

"Your future is contained in the other folios."

Archie replaced the first book on the shelf. There were two more with his name on their spines.

"Why are there two?" he asked.

"Because your path is uncertain."

"But which one should I choose?" demanded Archie, a note of desperation creeping into his voice.

"That is for you alone to decide. Two paths stand before you. One will keep you safe from harm, but if you follow it, you will not achieve your purpose, and magic will fade from the world. The second will allow you to wield great power and shape the future of magic. But it comes at a price."

"I will become a darchemist?" said Archie.

"You must choose," said the voice.

"That's not much of a choice," said Archie. "What if I reject both paths?"

"Then I cannot guarantee you have a future," said the voice.

Archie took a deep breath. "That is a chance I have to take," he said.

"You reject your destiny?" asked the voice.

"Yes, if it means letting magic die or becoming a darchemist, then I'd rather not have a future."

The voice was silent. Archie sensed that his life hung in the balance. He could feel his heart beating in his chest. The seconds ticked by, and then the voice spoke again. This time there was a note of surprise in it.

"Your father was right. He said that you would refuse both fates, even if it cost you your life. So look again, Archie Greene."

A fourth book had appeared on the shelf. Archie was

sure it hadn't been there before. He opened it. In its pages he saw himself standing before a large door. The image faded. He turned the page, but there was no more.

"The rest is blank!" he exclaimed, skimming through the pages.

"You chose the empty book. Its story has yet to be written. It is the least certain of the three. It is for you to forge. The choices you make will have consequences not just for you but also for the future of magic."

"I choose that path," cried Archie.

"Very well," said the voice. "Its ending is unknowable. But it is not blank. Look again."

Archie opened the book a second time. Something was slipped between the pages. It was a letter, and it was addressed to him in spidery handwriting similar to his own.

"It is from your father," the voice said. "He left it here for you to find."

Archie stared at the piece of paper in his hand. "But how . . . ?" he began.

"Fate is fickle, but none may cheat it," said the voice. "This way."

Archie took the letter and replaced the book on the shelf. As he turned to leave, he saw something on the shelf next to his own. Several faded books were covered with cobwebs, but one had recently been opened. The name on its spine was . . . Alexander Greene.

Archie's heart skipped a beat. He felt the tiny flame of hope that had been lit inside him suddenly flare.

"Wait," he cried. "You said that the folios contain the future. There is one for my father—does that mean he's alive?"

"You must hurry now," whispered the voice. "Time does not wait. The future is impatient."

"But you haven't answered my question," cried Archie. "I need to know if my father is alive or dead! And my mother and sister!"

Archie's heart was skittering madly. The sound of his own blood pumping in his head was deafening as he waited for an answer.

———

"Archie, wake up!"

Someone was shaking him. Archie opened his eyes to see Bramble's and Thistle's worried faces. He was lying on the floor of the Scriptorium. In one hand he gripped the Emerald Eye; in the other he clutched the letter.

He had no idea how he had escaped from *The Book of Prophecy* or got out of his retro-specter.

"My father left a message for me in *The Book of Prophecy*," he said.

In a daze, he read the letter.

Dear Archie,

If you are reading this, then my first plan has failed and you are in great danger. By now you know about the magical realm, and somehow you survived your encounter with Barzak.

You are probably wondering how I know these things. When you were born, I consulted the Books of Destiny, and they revealed to me that you have a forked fate.

The first fork was your meeting with Barzak. The second is less clear, but it is connected with Fabian Grey and the Alchemists' Curse. The third is hidden even from the Books of Destiny.

You are still a baby as I write this. I have spent every second since you were born searching for some way to help you avoid the second fork or stack the odds in your favor.

Tonight I will try to head off the danger or draw it to me. I leave this letter in case I fail and you must face the second trial alone.

*There is one more thing I must tell you. There
is a book that I found in Ripley's private library. It
contains information that can help you break the
curse. It is hidden with some books I left at Loretta's
house and is sealed with a magical clasp. Open it
with care and in the company of trusted friends.*

*Be brave, Archie. Much depends on you. And
remember, I am with you in spirit—always.*

Your loving father,
Alex Greene

Archie stared at the letter. His legs had turned to jelly.
So the book his father had taken from Ripley's collection
had something to do with the curse. Here at last was some
good news. He needed to find that book—and quickly.

———

As soon as he got home, Archie raced upstairs and took
out the old shoe box under his bed.

"Is it there?" asked Thistle, who had followed him.

Archie looked through his father's reference books.
There was *Magical Greats: The Good, the Bad, & the Ugly*,
and *Creatures to Avoid If You Are of a Nervous Disposition*.
There was the scrapbook with newspaper cuttings and
photographs. But that was all.

Archie's heart sank. Then he had another thought. He raced downstairs and into the kitchen. Thistle and Bramble trailed behind him.

"Aunt Loretta," he asked urgently, "did my dad ever give you any books to look after?"

"Not that I remember," said Loretta.

Archie felt his hopes dashed again.

"Wait a minute. Now that I think of it, he did give me a few books—cookery books. Can't think why," she added, disappearing into the larder. "Why would I need cookery books . . . ?"

Archie was no longer listening. He scanned the spines of the cookery books on the kitchen shelf.

He had almost given up when he spotted a book with no title on its spine. It looked different from the other cooking books. Archie climbed up on the kitchen counter and eased the book from the others. It was tatty-looking with a green cover and sealed with a clasp.

"Got it!" he declared.

"Got what?" asked Loretta's voice from the larder. But there was no reply.

The children had gone.

CHAPTER 20

The Book Ghast

Archie shivered. They were in Grey's laboratory and it was cold. Bramble had just lit a fire, and the three cousins were warming themselves.

Archie was thinking about what his father had said—that the book could help them break the curse. His mind had been racing ever since.

His thoughts were interrupted by the arrival of Arabella and Rupert. Arabella looked more pale and drawn than ever and she seemed on edge. "What's so urgent that you needed to call a special meeting?" she demanded. "Haven't we caused enough trouble with this club already?"

"Let's say the oath and then I'll tell you," Archie said.

Was it Archie's imagination or did Arabella look shifty when she said hers?

"My father took something from your grandfather's collection," he said, studying her face for a reaction. "It's the reason he had to leave the museum."

"What did he take?" she asked. Archie thought she looked frightened.

"It was a book," he said, holding it up for them to see. "He took it because he knew we'd need it. Perhaps it explains what happened to the original Alchemists' Club.

"I have a letter from my father. He told me to open the book around friends."

"What is it?" asked Rupert, reaching out to touch the journal. He pulled back his hand. "Where've you been keeping it, in a fridge? It's freezing!"

"Let me see it," said Arabella. She held the book in her hands and sniffed it. "It contains a spirit. We should hand it in to Hawke."

"No way!" said Bramble, taking the book from Arabella and giving it back to Archie. "Uncle Alex didn't hide it so that we could hand it over to Hawke."

"Bramble's right," said Archie. He took a deep breath. "I command you to open," he said, releasing the magical clasp so that the book fell open. A gray shadow reared up from between the pages, forming the shape of a man. The phantom looked like it was spun from the threads of a spider's web.

Its face creased into an angry scowl, and it drew back its pale, ghostly lips.

"How dare you disturb my unrest!" it snarled, and its bulging red eyes glared at them.

For a moment, they were all too shocked to answer. But Archie managed to gather himself.

"Your unrest?" he said. "Don't you mean we are disturbing your rest?"

The apparition shook its ghostly head. "I have no rest. I am *cursed.*" The creature hissed the word.

"It's a book ghast," Arabella said.

The book ghast made a hissing sound and nodded sadly. A mournful look replaced its angry expression. Now that it wasn't scowling, Archie thought there was something familiar about its features.

Arabella's brow creased in thought. "Ghasts are left behind for a reason. Something happened that means they can't move on. Usually it's some sort of tragic accident or unresolved issue."

"So, what happened to you?" Thistle asked the ghast. "Why are you still here?"

The ghast shimmered, and its translucent cobweb threads seemed to lose a little of their luster.

"There was an accident. My carriage overturned," it said miserably. "I was on my way to meet my friends, but I never got there."

"When was this?" asked Archie.

"It was just after the great fire. The year was 1666."

Archie had thought the ghast couldn't look any sadder, but now it seemed to have sunk even lower into its own misery. For a while, it did not speak. A look of deep concentration passed across its ghostly features, as if it was trying to recall some distant memory that was as faded as it was. Then it began to relate its sad story.

"I was an apprentice at the Museum of Magical Miscellany," it said, and its voice swelled with pride. "I was just a boy when I started, but I was determined to make my name. That's why I joined the Alchemists' Club. Fabian Grey was our leader and my best friend."

The ghast had a wistful look.

"We had such grand ideas. We were going to restore magic to its rightful place. That was our dream. We believed it was also our destiny.

"It was just talk to begin with. But then Fabian went a step further. He consulted *The Book of Prophecy*. We told him he shouldn't do it, but he just laughed."

"So Grey consulted *The Book of Prophecy* when he was still an apprentice at the museum?" asked Archie.

"Yes," said the ghast. "Fabian was fearless."

The ghast's face lit up for a moment, remembering happy times. But almost immediately its expression darkened.

"We thought it had killed him. It nearly did. Fabian was never the same after that. *The Book of Prophecy* changed him. Some of his hair turned white. He lost his mind for a while."

The ghast shook its head sadly. "Gradually, his memory returned, but he could not remember what he had learned in *The Book of Prophecy*, only that the future of magic rested on his shoulders and we were meant to help him."

Archie was starting to feel uncomfortable. The story sounded familiar. The similarities between him and Grey were becoming more and more clear.

But why had Grey been so affected by *The Book of Prophecy*, when he had not? Were his memories intact because he had the retro-specter to protect him? The ghast was still speaking.

"At that time England was ravaged by the plague. People were dying in the thousands. Fabian thought he could use magic to destroy the pestilence and make life better for people.

"We were already experimenting with magic by then. When the elders found out, they were angry because we hadn't consulted them. They expelled us from the museum, so we moved to London and rented the baker's cellar for our experiments. We started writing new magic. Just little spells at first. But Fabian said that if we could make Azoth, then we would be ready to rewrite the magical books."

"One day, Fabian told us he'd found the formula. He asked each of us to collect one of the ingredients. It was supposed to be our greatest triumph. But it all went terribly wrong. A sort of madness had taken hold of Felicia."

Archie remembered the scene he'd witnessed in *The Book of Yore.*

The ghost shook its ghostly head once more. "Everyone thought the fire had started in the bakery," the ghost went on. "But Thomas Farrinor told the king that we were to blame. We were disgraced. Worse than that—we were cursed, as are all those with the Golden Circle Firemark." The ghost had begun to fade.

"But how can we lift the curse?" asked Archie desperately.

"Everything you need to know is in the journal."

"Just one more thing," said Bramble. "What's your name?"

"I am the unfulfilled dream of Braxton Foxe," said the ghast. And with that it vanished.

The children crowded around the journal, trying to read over Archie's shoulder.

"It's Braxton Foxe's account of the days following the fire," said Archie. "The first entry is dated Monday, 4 September 1666—two days after the fire started. Listen to this.

"Even now the fire still smolders. They say that half of London is destroyed—and all because of us! We have received no word from Fabian. There are rumors that he was arrested in Oxford and imprisoned in the Tower of London.

"The story persists that the fire started in the baker's oven. If word gets out of our part in this, I fear for the safety of the magical realm. I worry that we have blackened the name of magic for all time. To think that we started the Alchemists' Club with the intention of saving magic, but have brought about its ruin. It is too much to bear. Yet it is our own fault. It was our arrogance and curiosity that brought us to this pass. If only we had not been so reckless. I believe we were in the grip of a sort of madness. If only we had thought of the consequences of our actions."

As the days passed, the entries took a more sinister turn. Archie read on aloud.

"22 September 1666
"It has been almost three weeks since that ill-fated day in the baker's cellar. There is still no word from Fabian. No word either from Felicia. Angelica, Roderick, and I remain in Oxford, where we are still trying to lie low. Yesterday, Roderick suffered a most unfortunate accident. A magical book released a scorpion, which stung him. He is expected to recover, but it gave him a nasty shock. No more than any of us deserve, I know.

"1 October 1666
"Roderick is dead. The scorpion sting proved fatal. Angelica and I have been summoned before the Council of Elders to account for our part in the great fire. Word is out in the magical realm that it was our doing. There is much talk about new Lores to prevent another magical conflagration occurring in the future. It seems that our attempts to restore magic to its rightful place may end up driving it underground.

"5 October 1666

"More bad news. Angelica is seriously ill. Some dark spell is upon her that robs her of her mind. The doctor has confined her to her bed. But she sleepwalks in the night. Last night she fell from a window. She was lucky to survive the fall. I hope that tomorrow brings better tidings.

"10 October 1666

"Angelica is dead. She had made a good recovery from her fall but was crushed to death when a stone gargoyle fell on her from a great height. I was with her at the time and narrowly escaped. There is more to these accidents than meets the eye. It is the curse!"

"12 October 1666

"At last, some good news! Word of Fabian! A letter arrived this morning from Felicia. She says Fabian has escaped from the Tower. They must have made up their differences, which is a great relief. I am to meet them. I am anxious to see my friends again. My carriage awaits—I leave immediately."

"That's the final entry," said Archie, closing the book.

"I think we know what happened next," said Rupert. "His carriage must have turned over on the way there. Roderick, Angelica, and then Braxton. All three of them were dead within a few weeks of the fire."

"That's what the Alchemists' Curse is—it's a curse on the members of the Alchemists' Club. Everyone who belongs to the club meets with an accident," said Archie.

"And the same thing is going to happen to us unless we can break the curse," said Arabella.

———

The next couple of days passed in a blur. Archie couldn't concentrate at work. He would have liked to confide in Old Zeb. But he knew that if he admitted that he'd consulted *The Book of Prophecy*, the old man would be duty bound to report him, so he said nothing.

Late one afternoon, the old bookbinder sent Archie to the museum on an errand. As he reached the Great Gallery, he saw Katerina walking puposefully toward Lost Books. He didn't feel like talking to her, so he turned off before she reached him. He opened the door and stepped into the Scriptorium. The torches blazed.

He wondered whether *The Book of Prophecy* would speak to him again.

"Hello," he said. "Can you hear me?"

Silence.

Archie walked up the short flight of stairs to the raised wooden platform that overlooked the Books of Destiny. He gazed at the glass dome holding the great books. Something was missing. *The Book of Charms* was gone. One of the elders must have moved it.

Archie looked down on the two remaining books. *The Book of Prophecy* was closed and silent. Archie's eyes roved from its gray jacket to the open pages of *The Book of Reckoning*.

"Each and every one of us will pass through its pages," Bramble had told him the very first time he'd visited the Scriptorium. Right now that seemed more poignant to Archie than ever.

Column after column of names filled its pages. Beside each entry was their date of birth and another space to record their death. The blue Bennu bird quill floated in the air just above its open pages, scribbling entries and constantly updating itself. As he watched, it wrote out a new name, *Cecilia Scrivens*. Archie felt a momentary sense of joy that a baby had been born to a magical family.

But then, immediately, the pages flicked backward. The quill hovered over an earlier entry—*Jacob Merryfellow, born 23 December 1932*—and added the word *died* and the date. Then it put a single line through the name.

Archie had a sudden thought.

"They must be recorded in there," he said aloud. "The original members of the Alchemists' Club. Braxton Foxe and the rest."

At the sound of the name of Braxton Foxe, *The Book of Reckoning* started to glow with a yellow light. The pages turned backward, gathering speed until they were just a blur, and then suddenly stopped. The blue quill hovered above a faded entry. There was a single line through the name, but Archie could still read it.

Braxton Thistle Foxe: Born 26 November 1649—died 12 October 1666.

It confirmed what they had already guessed. Braxton Foxe had died the same day as his last entry in the journal.

Archie heard the door open quietly behind him. He turned to see Bramble silhouetted in the doorway. "I thought you might be here," she said gently.

"They were so young," said Archie sadly.

"I know," said Bramble. "Not very much older than we are now."

Archie glanced over at the painting. Until that moment the alchemists in the picture had seemed so grown-up.

"All that potential," said Bramble, shaking her head.

"And Fabian Grey," said Archie, sighing, "the most talented of all."

The blue Bennu quill moved again, coming to rest above a faded name.

Fabian Grey: Born 18 August 1649. There was no date for Grey's death.

But neither Archie nor Bramble noticed, because as they were looking at it, a light had just gone on inside the painting. The door at the back of the room had opened and a hooded figure was moving toward the table. Archie stared at the figure.

"Do you understand now, book whisperer?" hissed *The Book of Prophecy.* "It is the door to the Darchive . . . and the door to your destiny."

The color drained from Archie's face. Finally, it was all starting to make sense. It had been right in front of him all along. The prophecy in the painting was coming true.

"The darchemist is here!" he cried. "In the Darchive!"

CHAPTER 21

The Confession

W e have to get into the Darchive!" Archie blurted out when he and Bramble saw Thistle and Rupert a short while later. "There's something hidden in the Darchive, and the darchemist has come for it."

"But what is it?" asked Thistle.

"It's what Arthur Ripley discovered in there. I think it's one of the Terrible Tomes," said Archie, "and I think I know which one!"

"We have to tell Hawke," said Rupert.

"He's gone to London to see Arthur Ripley again," said Bramble.

"Well, Graves, then," said Rupert.

"There's no time," said Archie. "The darchemist is already in there!"

"What are we going to do?"

Archie didn't reply immediately; he was thinking. Someone inside the museum had wanted the dark spell to be written all along. And now the darchemist had come to finish it.

"We have to break the curse or the museum will be destroyed—and us with it. Where's Arabella?"

He had a horrible thought. Could Arabella be the darchemist? At that moment, she appeared from the direction of Hawke's office.

"There you are, Arabella," Archie cried. "Where have you been?"

"I was standing on the stairs," she replied. "I overheard everything."

Her eyes had welled up with tears. "This is all my fault," she sobbed.

Archie stared at her. "What's your fault?" he asked.

"I was the one who opened the Grabber."

"No one blames you for that," said Bramble.

Arabella paused, her lip quivering. "But there's something else you don't know. I was the one who sent Rupert the locket."

"What?" cried Rupert angrily. "You sent me a hexed Keep Safe? Why?"

"I found it among my grandfather's things. I was trying to scare you."

"Scare me," said Rupert. "It nearly killed me!"

"Yes, I know," sniffed Arabella, tears streaming down her pale face now. "I didn't think it would be so strong. I just wanted to give you a fright.

"Grey and the other alchemists were taken over by a sort of madness. Magic does that to people. I've seen it in my family. My grandfather is a Greader, and my parents aren't much better. I didn't want that to happen to us. I thought if I scared you with the curse, it would save us from that."

She turned to Archie. "I'm so sorry. Now I've ruined everything. If I hadn't sabotaged the club, you might have been able to stop them."

She paused. "I don't blame you if you don't want me as a member anymore."

"What about Gloom and the black quill—was that you as well?" asked Bramble.

"No!" cried Arabella. "I was trying to stop you writing magic."

Archie gazed at Arabella's tear-streaked face. He desperately wanted to believe her. In her own strange and misguided way, she had been trying to protect them.

"Let's put it to a vote," said Archie. "All those in favor of Arabella remaining in the Alchemists' Club?"

Three hands went up. Rupert hesitated and then raised his hand, too.

"I'd say that's pretty conclusive," said Bramble.

"Thank you," said Arabella, drying her eyes. "I won't let you down again."

"Good," said Archie. "Because we've got a museum to save, and we'll need your help."

When they reached the Darchive, the door was open. The five children stepped inside.

⌒

At that moment, in another part of the museum, Feodora Graves was framed in the doorway of the Scriptorium. Morag Pandrama and Wolfus Bone were just behind her.

"Archie? Bramble? Thistle? Rupert? Arabella? Where are you?" cried Graves.

"Look!" cried Bone, staring at the painting. "The door in the picture is open! It must be some sort of portal."

"I can see them!" cried Pandrama, pointing to where five figures had just appeared in the painting. "I recognize the door. They're inside the Darchive!"

As they watched it, the picture filled with gray mist.

When it cleared, the painting had changed. Where the five original alchemists had sat there were five empty chairs around the table.

"It's the prophecy," gasped Graves. "It's coming true."

———

Ahead of them, the five children could see a light. As they walked toward it, they smelled burning incense. Archie clutched the Emerald Eye in one hand, glad of the little bit of light that it gave off. The air was close now. The thick white vapor filled the air with a pungent scent. It was making them feel drowsy.

They could feel some hypnotic force drawing them on. Archie's mind was emptying. He tried to fight it, but it was too strong.

———

In the Scriptorium, Graves and Pandrama watched the children's progress, unable to take their eyes off the painting. They saw the five children approaching the table. A cloaked figure stepped out from the shadows.

"Someone is expecting them," said Graves.

She stared at the picture, willing the five apprentices to turn around and go back the way they'd come.

Aurelius Rusp burst into the Scriptorium. "We've just heard that Arthur Ripley has escaped from the asylum.

He may be heading this way. There's a crowd gathering outside Quill's."

"Greaders!" cried Graves, suddenly snapping into action. "They're going to attack the museum. Tell Pink to lock the Door Ray! Let's just hope the Permission Wall holds. Aurelius, go to Natural Magic and warn Motley. And find Orpheus."

Graves paused. "Where is Gideon?"

"He's not back from London," said Pandrama.

"Very well," Graves continued. "Morag, you stay here. I will try to reach them in the Darchive. Now, everybody move."

The five children walked toward the light. No one had spoken since they'd stepped over the threshold into the Darchive. The incense was making them drowsy, filling their heads and stopping them from thinking.

Ahead of them, they could see the outline of a table with five empty chairs. On the table there were two books—one with a red-and-gold cover and the other black. Next to the books was the black quill and a crystal inkwell that glowed with a golden light.

A cloaked figure beckoned them forward. Archie felt light-headed, like he might faint. Rupert, Bramble, and

Arabella stepped past him. Rupert stumbled into the light. As he did, he looked into the hooded face.

"Oh," he said. "It's you."

The cloaked figure pointed at a chair and then at the black book. Rupert sat down.

Arabella followed. "How did you get here?" she asked. The cloaked figure gestured toward another chair and then toward the black book. Arabella took her place at the table.

"I should have guessed," murmured Bramble when it was her turn. But she, too, sat at the table and glanced toward the black book.

"Arch," whispered Thistle. "My ring is glowing. It's a trap. . . ."

But it was too late: Thistle had already taken his place at the table.

Archie reached for the Emerald Eye and grasped it in his hand. His breath was coming in shallow, wheezy gasps now. His brain was beginning to play tricks on him. He felt something drawing him toward the table.

He stepped into the light. As soon as he did, he felt the atmosphere around him change. Everything had become dreamlike. It must be the incense, he thought, or some enchantment on the place.

"Rupert? Bramble? Arabella? Thistle?" he called.

But there was no reply.

The hooded figure stood just in front of him.

"Who are you?" demanded Archie. "What have you done to my friends?"

The figure turned and walked toward the black book on the table.

The air shimmered and shapes began to materialize around him. Gradually the objects in the room became more solid until Archie could see them clearly. He recognized the scene from the painting, but where the original members of the Alchemists' Club had been before, his four friends sat frozen like statues in the exact same poses.

With a jolt, he realized that the prophecy had always been about them. But Grey had painted himself looking away.

"Your seat is prepared," the cloaked figure said, pointing at the fifth chair, which was empty. The voice sounded familiar, but Archie couldn't place it. He felt his eyes drawn to the book. He fought the urge to look.

He heard Gloom's words in his head. *The Emerald Eye will protect you from magical books, even the dark ones, as long as you don't look directly at them.*

Archie forced himself to look away. He took a deep breath to try to clear his head.

"My name is Archie Greene, and I am an apprentice bookbinder at the Museum of Magical Miscellany," he declared, mustering all the courage he could find.

"I know who you are, book whisperer," said the cloaked figure. "You are expected." She threw back her cloak, and Archie gazed into the deep blue eyes of Katerina Krone.

"But I don't understand," said Archie. "What are you doing here?"

"I have come to claim my inheritance," said Katerina. "The Nightshade inheritance!

"Felicia Nightshade was my ancestor. She had great plans. If only that little fire hadn't started."

"Little fire!" exclaimed Archie. "It burned down half of London!"

"It was nothing next to what Felicia would have achieved," snapped Katerina. "And now we can finish her work. We can complete the Unfinished Spell."

"But what does it do?" asked Archie, a deep sense of unease settling on him.

"The Unfinished Spell will allow Hecate's powers to pass to her descendant," said Katerina.

Archie swallowed hard. He now knew for certain which book it was—*The Grim Grimoire*. It was the *Grimoire* that had spoken to him in the Darchive, and it was the *Grimoire* that had tried to use the children to bring its dark magic back into the world.

A cold dread gripped him. "You're going to finish Hecate's spell?" he said.

"No," laughed Katerina. "You are!"

CHAPTER 22

The Darchemist

The *Grimoire* is a family heirloom. If it hadn't been for that fool Grey, Hecate's powers would have been passed down long ago," sneered Katerina.

"Generations of Nightshades tried to complete the spell." She gave a bitter laugh. "But none of them succeeded in writing magic. Not until Felicia. She befriended Fabian Grey at the museum. She knew that once she had the Golden Circle Firemark, all she had to do was stay close to Grey and he would do the rest.

"Grey wanted to rewrite the books of magic. How virtuous! But that was never Felicia's intention. She played along with their silly Alchemists' Club, biding her time.

And when the moment arrived, she was ready. How was she to know that Grey would rather destroy his own life's work than let her finish the spell?"

"And that's why the *Grimoire* cursed them?"

Katerina laughed aloud. "Oh yes. That was its revenge. One by one they were struck down in mysterious ways. Everything was working out perfectly—except for Grey! You see, he took the *Grimoire* from the cellar in Pudding Lane.

"The last thing he did before he was taken to the Tower was hide it somewhere he thought it would never see the light of day. And then he did his vanishing trick. Curse him!

"The *Grimoire* was lost for three hundred and fifty years, until Arthur Ripley went looking for secrets in the Darchive and found it where Grey had left it. Or rather it found him! The *Grimoire* does that. It draws people to it.

"Being a Ripley, of course, Arthur saw the potential in the situation. He knew that the Firemarks would appear exactly three hundred and fifty years after the first Alchemists' Club. All he had to do was track down the next Nightshade in line to inherit. Me!"

"But you're a Krone, not a Nightshade," said Archie.

"My parents died when I was very young, and I was

adopted by the Krones. 'Nice' people, if you like that sort of thing. Personally, I don't! No ambition and very narrow-minded about dark magic.

"So Ripley traced me and wrote to my adopted parents about my inheritance. They weren't going to tell me, but they kept the letter. That was their mistake. Imagine how angry I was when I found it! All I needed to do was find a way to complete the spell and Hecate's powers would be mine.

"I was just a child then, too young to act. So I pleaded with my parents to let me come to the museum when I was twelve. I can be very persuasive when I want to be. They finally relented—but I failed the Flame test! Can you believe it? So I made it my mission to learn everything I could about writing magic. They all thought I was such a good student. Little did they realize my real motive. It wasn't until I won the scholarship to the musem that they became suspicious. That's when they had to go."

"The couple in Prague?" gasped Archie.

"Yes, they found Grey's notebook among my things. Felicia took it from the burning cellar, and it was passed down to me. The Krones were going to hand it in to the museum. They tipped off Hawke, and he arranged to have it collected. I couldn't allow them to do that, so they had to die. I arranged for Roach to pay them a visit, but they realized what I'd done. By the time Roach arrived in Prague to collect the notebook, they'd already got rid of it. They thought they were clever, sending it to poor old Aunt Flora in Edinburgh. So Roach had to pay her a visit. The silly woman refused to hand it over at first, said she'd report it, so she had to die, too."

"So you already had the notebook," said Archie, shocked by her calousness. "You just pretended to find it in Grey's laboratory. I thought it was suspicious that we didn't find it when we went through Grey's papers."

"Yes, and with my relatives out of the way, I was free to come to the musem. And then the Firemarks started to appear again. So I waited for mine. I was sure it would come. But it never did. Ripley, Trevallen, the Foxes—and worst of all, Fabian Grey's descendant—Archie Greene! You all got the mark except for me, who needed it most."

"That's why you were so unhappy about the Firemarks. You weren't concerned for our safety—you just wanted one so you could write magic."

Katerina laughed. "I already had Felicia's quill and the formula for Azoth. I just needed the Firemark. But when it didn't happen, I needed another plan.

"And there you were with your forked fate. It was too

good an opportunity to miss.

"The *Grimoire* drew you and your cousin to it once I had bewitched the Dragon's Claw."

"That was you?"

"Of course."

"And it was you who sent the Grabber that Arabella opened?"

"Yes. I couldn't take the chance that you would actually succeed in rewriting *The Book of Charms*. That would have spoiled everything."

"Because you needed access to the Darchive," said Archie. He needed to keep Katerina talking until he could think of a plan.

"Once the spell is complete, Hecate's powers will pass to me and I will be the next great darchemist, but I needed a magic writer—and here you are! Now take your seat and we can begin."

Katerina glanced across at the black book on the table. Archie felt it drawing his eyes to it. He fought the urge to look.

"Still you resist it," said Katerina with a cruel smile, "but not for much longer. Soon its power will be unopposed. The charms protecting the museum are almost gone."

She glanced at *The Book of Charms* on the table.

"The old magic that protects the museum is stronger than you realize," said Archie, repeating what Hawke had said. "It has lasted a thousand years, and it will outlast you."

He said it more out of defiance than real conviction.

Katerina laughed. "*The Grim Grimoire* is the greatest book of magic ever written. You will do as the *Grimoire* commands."

"Silence!" said a voice that crackled and spat like fat on a fire. It was the voice he had heard before in the Darchive. It was coming from the black book.

"I am *The Grim Grimoire*, the book of darkness."

"And I am Hecate's blood relation," cried Katerina. "You will be mine."

"No," spat the *Grimoire*. "You have played your part by bringing the book whisperer to me. Did you really think that you would be strong enough to possess me? Fool! You are too weak to be a darchemist. You cannot even write magic!

"It is Grey's blood that I crave. Archie Greene will be the next darchemist."

"No!" roared Katerina. "I am the one who will inherit. It's my birthright. I am Hecate's heir. You will obey me!"

A peal of high, mocking laughter rent the air. "You would dare to defy me?" cackled the *Grimoire*. "Fool!"

There was a blinding flash of light. Archie staggered backward, his heart pounding. When he looked again, Katerina's body had gone limp. Her eyes had rolled back in her head and she appeared to be dead.

"And now, Archie Greene," sneered the *Grimoire*, "it is time for you to fulfill your true destiny by completing the Unfinished Spell."

CHAPTER 23

The Unfinished Spell

Inside the Scriptorium, Morag Pandrama watched in horror as the events inside the Darchive unfolded before her eyes. The torches inside the Scriptorium had not ignited. She was on the third candle by now and was beginning to lose hope.

Just before midnight, Brown arrived with Gloom. When Graves joined them a little later, Loretta and Woodbine Foxe were with her. On hearing them enter the room, Pandrama turned with expectant eyes.

Graves gave a weak smile. "We have done all that we can," she said, sighing. "The door to the Darchive is locked on the inside, but Gideon and Wolfus are trying to open it. Now we must wait and hope."

As she said it, the last candle went out and they were suddenly aware that the only light in the room was the dim glow coming from the painting. At that moment that light went out, too, plunging the Scriptorium into total darkness.

"What happened?" cried Loretta, her voice trembling.

All they could see now was a tiny speck of light in the picture. Loretta stared at the dot of light, willing it to stay on, afraid that if she looked away even for a second, she would never find it again. It was no more than a speck on the canvas, but she was not going to let it out of her sight. None of them were.

⟶

In the Darchive, Archie watched in horror as Katerina's limp body rose from the ground like some grotesque puppet and picked up the black book from the table. Archie heard a low, cackling sound and realized the *Grimoire* was laughing.

He stepped backward until he felt the wall behind him and could go no farther.

"Finish the spell," demanded the *Grimoire*.

"And if I refuse?" cried Archie.

The *Grimoire* gave a high-pitched laugh. "If you refuse

me, then you will suffer the same fate as your father!"

"My father?" cried Archie, unable to believe what he was hearing. "You know where he is?"

"I know he is trapped inside a book," sneered the *Grimoire*. "Ripley saw to that. And now it is your turn. I will imprison you until you beg to do my will."

It laughed again in a cold, cruel voice. "There is no one to save you!"

Archie looked desperately at his friends, frozen like waxwork dummies at the table. It was his fault. It was his recklessness that had led them into danger. And now he could do nothing to help them or to save the museum.

The *Grimoire* was right—he was alone.

His mind was reeling. If only he could think of a way to free the others, at least they might escape. The *Grimoire* had made a mistake by telling him that Ripley had imprisoned his father. It meant to break his spirit and crush his resistance. But it had the opposite effect. Archie was fired up with anger.

"Take me and release the others," he cried.

"Your life for theirs?" cackled the *Grimoire*. "How delicious. Your father offered to trade his life for yours. But it did him no good. His sacrifice was futile. All such sacrifice is. You must see that now, surely? That's why you will join us and become a darchemist.

"The Unfinished Spell will give you the power you need to fulfill your destiny—the power to save magic. The strong shall inherit from the weak. Finish the spell!"

The *Grimoire* flipped open on the table. The black quill and the inkwell were next to it. All he had to do was pick up the quill, dip it in the Azoth.

"Do it," urged the *Grimoire*. "Finish the spell!"

Still Archie hesitated.

"You have no choice," said the *Grimoire*, laughing. "If you will not do it for yourself, then you will do it to save your friends. If you do not write the magic, then they will remain as they are—forever."

Archie stared at the quill on the table, his mind racing. He looked at Bramble and Thistle and reached out for the quill. His hand was shaking.

He saw a look of horror in Bramble's frozen eyes. She could see and hear what was happening. They both knew that if he wrote the dark magic to complete the spell, he would become a darchemist, but he had no choice.

"Sorry, Bram," he mumbled.

His fingers brushed the black quill. He felt his palm itch, and the Golden Circle Firemark began to glow. As it did, he felt something twitch in his pocket. It was the ring. He had forgotten it was there. He pulled back his hand and took the ring from his pocket. He held it on his open palm. It fitted his Firemark perfectly. He remembered the words written inside the ring and murmured them to himself.

> *"This is my word, this is my mark*
> *Forged in the fire, a light in the dark."*

To his surprise, the ring pulsed, and Archie watched in amazement as the circle of gold sprang open and uncurled so that the dragon's head and tail separated. As it straightened, the fins of a feather unfurled. Where the ring had been just a moment before, Archie stared at the golden quill sitting on the palm of his hand.

Finally, he knew the ring's secret. Hidden within it was Fabian Grey's golden Bennu quill. He grasped it and felt it twitch in his hand. He plunged the quill into the Azoth.

And as he did, gold fiery letters appeared above his head.

Book of charms, strong and true
With this spell I renew!

The *Book of Charms* on the table next to the *Grimoire* flew open, and the faded spells began to darken until they were visible once more.

"What is this?" cried the *Grimoire*. "Grey's quill! So you have restored *The Book of Charms*. What do I care? It is the dawn of a new dark age of magic. You are Grey's heir. You would have made the most powerful darchemist. But if you will not write the spell, then others must be made to! The Ripley girl will serve as well."

Arabella woke from her frozen state. Archie could see a look of panic in her eyes, but the *Grimoire* was controlling her just as it had controlled Katerina.

Arabella picked up the black quill and began to write in *The Grim Grimoire*.

Black fiery letters appeared above her head.

In dark places where none may go
Shadows linger from long ago
Secrets lurk from older days
Hidden paths and stealthy ways.

Some have tried to find their way
To make the darkness go away . . .

Archie pushed Arabella aside. Grasping the golden quill tightly, he scribbled an ending to the spell.

Flame of Pharos guide my verse
Break the spell and lift the curse.

A ball of fire shot from the golden quill and engulfed the Unfinished Spell.

"What is this?" snarled the *Grimoire*. "It is too late to change what has already been written."

"'No," cried Archie. "It is never too late." With a final flourish of the quill, he wrote,

Book of darkness, book of black
In the name of Pharos, I cast you back!

A golden flame danced across the open pages of the *Grimoire*. For a moment it flared and burned, and the black book crackled with its heat. And then the black letters that formed its spells turned to dust and blew away on the breeze, leaving the pages empty.

Archie heard someone cry out, and he turned to see Gideon Hawke and Wolfus Bone running toward him. Hawke slammed the black book closed and Bone fixed a magical clasp on it.

"The dark spells are destroyed," said Archie.

"Are you all right?" asked Hawke, concern etched onto his face.

Archie felt a huge wave of relief well up inside him. He had been so caught up in the events of the last few hours that he had not realized how exhausted he was.

"It was Katerina all along," he said. "She was working with the Greaders. They were trying to finish Hecate's spell."

"Yes," said Hawke, holding his head. "I should have realized sooner.

"I went to see Ripley again to try to convince him to tell me what he knew. But when I got to the asylum, he'd escaped. I guessed an attack was imminent, so I raced back as fast as I could. I arrived just in time to hear that you had gone into the Darchive."

At that moment a sound behind them made him turn. Bramble, Thistle, and Rupert stood up.

"Archie!" cried Bramble. "Thank goodness you're all right."

They gathered around him, hugging him and slapping him on the back.

Wolfus Bone examined Katerina. Her face was white, her eyes vacant. "So much for the Nightshade inheritance," he said, wrapping a blanket around her shoulders.

"I've seen that look before," said Hawke grimly. "I'll contact the asylum and ask Rumold to collect her."

"The Book of Prophecy said that no one can cheat their fate," said Archie.

"Not even Fabian Grey," added Hawke under his breath.

At that moment, Archie noticed Arabella still sitting. She was staring at *The Grim Grimoire*, a look of confusion on her face, the black quill still gripped in her hand.

"Arabella," cried Archie. "Are you all right?"

She nodded. "Yes. I think so."

CHAPTER 24

Fabian Grey's Secret

"To think that Braxton Foxe's journal was with my cookery books all that time," said Loretta, shaking her head. "I would never have guessed."

The five members of the Alchemists' Club were sitting around the kitchen table at number 32 Houndstooth Road. The table was covered with plates of sandwiches, bowls of chips, and all manner of cakes and buns.

Loretta had insisted that they all come back for a very late Foxe feast. The children hadn't taken much persuading. Gideon Hawke, Feodora Graves, and Orpheus Gloom were also there.

"Yes, Mum," said Thistle, "that's why it was such a

good hiding place. Uncle Alex knew it would be safe there."

"So there really was something dark in the Darchive!" said Loretta.

"Yes," said Hawke. "And books don't get much darker than *The Grim Grimoire*."

"The Greaders who had gathered outside the museum all dispersed as soon as the *Grimoire* was defeated," said Graves. "Amos Roach is wanted for the murder of Katerina's parents and aunt. He will be brought to justice."

"And Arthur Ripley?" asked Archie.

"Still on the loose, I'm afraid," said Graves. "But not for long. Word is out in the magical realm—he will be recaptured."

"And rest assured, we will find out what he knows about your father's disappearance," said Hawke, placing his hand on Archie's shoulder. "If he is still alive, we will find him. I give you my word."

"Well, in honor of Alex, I've used a recipe from one of the cookery books he gave me," declared Loretta. She opened the door to the walk-in larder. "Strange ingredients. But I suppose it's good to experiment."

Gloom turned pale at the mention of an experiment.

"What I don't understand is why the *Grimoire* didn't curse Fabian Grey as well," said Archie.

"It did," said Hawke.

"So why didn't he die with the others?"

"Because there are worse ways to be cursed."

"Do you think we will ever find out what happened to him?" Archie asked.

But before anyone could answer, Loretta emerged from the larder carrying a very large cake. "It's banana and walnut," she declared.

"Just banana and walnut?" asked Thistle suspiciously.

"Yes," said Loretta.

Five hands reached for a slice and five mouths took a big bite.

"And some sardines, obviously . . . ," added Loretta. "More elderberry squash, anyone?"

⟶

At that very same moment, some fifty miles away at the London offices of Folly & Catchpole, Horace Catchpole stared at the open ledger in front of him. He read the entry again for the umpteenth time, but it still made no sense to him.

Someone coughed.

"Catchpole?" Prudence Folly said. "You wanted to

show me something? Have you found any more refer-
ences to the boy, Archie Greene?"

Horace shook his head firmly. "No," he said. "But . . .
well, it's this entry. Most irregular."

Prudence raised one manicured eyebrow. She glanced
at the entry. It said:

Property of Fabian Grey.

Do NOT remove.

Owner will collect.

Mudberry's Magical Glossary

The following excerpts are reproduced from Mudberry's *A Beginner's Guide to Magic* (13th Edition), with grateful thanks to the Mudberry family.

Agatha's Emporium: a magical shop in Oxford that sells astroscopes and other magical memorabilia. It is one of the best-known magical stores, along with the Flaming Tattoo Parlor, Mother Marek's Musical Muffins, and Veruca's Secret.

Aisle of White: the magical bookshop attached to the Museum of Magical Miscellany. The Aisle of White serves as a place to sort the magical books from other books that people come to sell, and is the only part of the museum open to the Unready. Its current proprietor is Geoffrey Screech.

The Alchemists' Club: a group of seventeenth-century

alchemists led by Fabian Grey, who tried to rewrite the magical books contained in the Museum of Magical Miscellany. Their magical experiments started the Great Fire of London and led to the introduction of the Lores of Magical Restraint. *Their experiments also triggered the Alchemists' Curse.*

Alchemists' Firemark: the symbol of a golden dragon swallowing its own tail (also known as the Golden Circle Firemark). The appearance of the Firemark indicates that an apprentice is able to write magic. It is also the symbol of the Alchemists' Club.

Amora: the smell of magic. Different types of magic give off different amoras. Natural Magic smells of nature. Mortal Magic smells of fusty rooms and fire smoke. And Supernatural Magic smells of cold tombs and dead flesh.

Apprenticeships: The magical apprenticeships were developed as a way to pass on the magical knowledge to the next generation. The Flame of Pharos determines the order in which an apprentice learns the three book skills:

- Finding (Firemark symbol: eye)
- Binding (Firemark: needle and thread)
- Minding (Firemark: ladder)

Archive: located in the Lost Books Department at the Museum of Magical Miscellany. The Archive is where all the old texts relating to magical books are kept. The texts date back to the Great Library of Alexandria and the Golden Age of Magic that preceded it.

Azoth: A magical substance highly prized by alchemists. It is one of the three requirements for writing magic. The other two are the Golden Circle Firemark and an enchanted quill made from a feather given freely by a magical creature. The ancient magic writers wrote their master spells with Azoth because of its long-lasting properties. It can also extend the life expectancy of mortals. The symbol for Azoth is the caduceus.

Barzak: The most feared darchemist of his time, Barzak wrote *The Book of Souls*, one of the seven Terrible Tomes, and was responsible for burning down the Great Library of Alexandria. He was subsequently imprisoned in *The Book of Souls* by Archie Greene.

Bookend Beasts: ancient stone griffins that guard magical books and artifacts. They can be identified by their amber eyes and can come to life if the secrets they protect are threatened. Bookend Beasts are extremely loyal and able to perform remarkable feats of magic. The last known pair protected the magic books in the

Great Library of Alexandria. Highly dangerous: do not approach.

Bookery: the great vaulted space between Quill's and the entrance to the Museum of Magical Miscellany, where magical books roost in huge bookcases like birds or fly around in flocks.

Books of Destiny: the name given to *The Book of Prophecy* and *The Book of Reckoning*. *The Book of Yore* is also sometimes included.

Book Whisperer: one who can talk to magical books, a very rare magical ability. Archie Greene is the first book whisperer in four hundred years.

Darchemist: writer of dark magic, including the authors of the Terrible Tomes.

Darchive: a secret place in the Museum of Magical Miscellany that is kept in total darkness. The Darchive houses magical books and artifacts that must never see the light of day. A number of dark magical items are stored there. Over the years several famous and infamous members of the magical realm have gained access to the Darchive. In the seventeenth century, the alchemist Fabian Grey is known to have visited on at least one occasion. The last known visitor was Arthur Ripley.

Door Ray: the secret entrance to the back of house in Quill's Coffee & Chocolate House. The Door Ray provides access the Museum of Magical Miscellany. It is disguised as a sunbeam to confuse the Unready.

Dragon's Claw: is one of the oldest Seats of Learning. The Dragon's Claw belonged to Fellwind the Destroyer, one of the great dragons of the North. Its claw was so large that it could hold two men, which is why the Dragon's Claw is one of a small number of double seats. The Dragon's Claw has a reputation for trickery and treachery.

Drawing Books: highly dangerous magical books that draw unwary readers into their pages. They include *The Book of Yore*, the history of magic.

Emerald Eye: the magical pendant that belonged to the magician John Dee, and that Dee's ghost gave to Archie Greene as his Keep Safe.

Enchanted Entrance: a secret doorway underneath the Aisle of White that gives access to other magical places.

Firemark: a magical symbol that appears on the palm of an apprentice's hand when he or she passes the Flame test. New Firemarks appear when the Flame of Pharos determines an apprentice is ready for the next challenge.

Flame Keepers of Alexandria: a secret community devoted to finding and preserving magical books. The Flame Keepers protect the Museum of Magical Miscellany in Oxford and are descended from the original guardians of the Great Library of Alexandria.

Flame of Pharos: The Flame of Pharos burned in the lighthouse in the harbor of Alexandria, guiding travelers from faraway lands to the books. When the Great Library of Alexandria burned down, the Flame was brought to Oxford. Legend has it that the flame contains the spirits of the Magisters, the ancient magic writers from the Golden Age of Magic, and is the conscience of the magical realm. The Flame now burns in the Word Smithy in the Mending Workshop beneath the Aisle of White and marks new apprentices with a Firemark for the three apprentice skills: Finding, Minding, or Binding.

Folly & Catchpole: the oldest and most secretive law firm in England. Folly & Catchpole has been the legal firm of choice for the magical community of Britain for more than nine hundred years. Based in London, just off Fleet Street, it specializes in magical instructions and the storage of magical items and other secrets.

Forbidden Books: magical books that must not be opened.

They include the Terrible Tomes and other books that are covered under prohibited practices.

Golden Age of Magic: most people have forgotten about magic or don't know it ever existed. But long ago there was a Golden Age when magic was practiced openly. In those days, master magicians called Magisters wrote the master spells that magicians have relied on ever since. As long as the master spell remains intact, someone else trained in magic can cast the spell by speaking it.

Greaders: sworn enemies of the Flame Keepers. In secret they still use magic for their own purposes and ignore the Lores of Magical Restraint. They are called Greaders because they are greedy for magical books and will go to any lengths to get their hands on them. The apprentices who work at the museum have to be always on their guard against them. Above all else the Greaders desire the Terrible Tomes.

Great Library of Alexandria: the most famous library of all time, it housed the greatest collection of magical books ever assembled. The library was burned down in around 48 BC.

Happy Landing: the place just outside the main doors to the Museum of Magical Miscellany, where the Seats of Learning deposit visitors.

Hecate Nightshade: a darchemist. Hecate was a witch who wrote *The Grim Grimoire*, a book of diabolical spells, which is one of the seven Terrible Tomes. According to legend, a bolt of lightning killed Hecate as she was trying to complete the final spell, giving rise to its name, the Unfinished Spell.

John Dee (1527–1609): Dee was an English mathematician, astronomer, astrologer, alchemist, and navigator. One of the most learned men of his age, Dee was Queen Elizabeth I's court magician and amassed one of the largest private libraries in Europe, including many rare and magical books. Dee's ghost gave his favorite scrying crystal pendant, the Emerald Eye, to Archie Greene as a Keep Safe.

Keep Safe: a magical gift usually given to someone to protect them from danger. Traditionally, you receive a Keep Safe from a friend or family member when you start your magical apprenticeship.

Lost Books Department: located in the Museum of Magical Miscellany, the Lost Books Department identifies magical books that have gone astray. When a new book arrives, it first goes to Lost Books to be classified according to its magical strength. Former heads of

Lost Books include the Greader Arthur Ripley. The current head is Gideon Hawke.

Magic: There are three branches of magic.

- **Natural Magic:** the purest kind of magic. It comes from magical creatures and plants and the elemental forces of nature, such as the sun, the stars, and the seas. (Symbol: tree with lightning bolt)
- **Mortal Magic:** man-made magic. It includes the magical instruments and other devices created by magicians to channel magical power. (Symbol: crystal ball)
- **Supernatural Magic:** the third and darkest type of magic. It uses the power of spirits and other supernatural beings. (Symbol: smiling skull)

Magician's Eye: the condition of having eyes that are different colors. Magician's Eye is associated with rare magical abilities, including a talent for dark magic.

Magister: master magician and magic writer from the Golden Age of Magic.

Motion Potion: an antigravity potion served at Quill's that is required to travel safely in the Seats of Learning. Motion Potions come in a variety of flavors and names and can be mixed with hot chocolate (choc-tails) or fruit juices.

Museum of Magical Miscellany: the secret building concealed under the Bodleian Library in Oxford that houses the world's most powerful magical books. All magical books must be returned to the museum for inspection and classification.

Opus Magus: written during the Golden Age of Magic, the Opus Magus is the great work of magic. It contains the founding spells that created magic itself.

Permission Wall: an enchantment that disguises magical places so they can't be seen from the outside. Typically a secret mark or password is required as "permission" to pass through the Permission Wall.

Poppers: magical books with spells that can escape if they are opened. There are two types: Pop-Ups are spells that can escape from a book but must remain with it. Pop-Outs are able to roam freely.

Popper Stopper: a glass phial which, when uncorked, releases a white vapor that surrounds and captures wayward Popper spells. Once used, a Popper Stopper must be returned to the museum so that the spell it contains can be put back into its book or disposed of in some other way. First and Second Hand apprentices are forbidden to use Popper Stoppers, because they are deemed too dangerous.

Quill's Coffee & Chocolate House: founded in London in 1657 by Jacob Quill, Quill's became a favorite meeting place for the magical community. In 1667, Quill's moved to Oxford after the original shop was destroyed in the Great Fire of London. It has been in Oxford ever since. As well as its internationally famous choc-tails, it boasts one of the most impressive Permission Walls anywhere in the magical world, which acts as the entrance to the Museum of Magical Miscellany.

Royal Society of Magic: Founded in 1666 by King Charles II, the Royal Society was established to further the understanding of magic. Its mission is to recognize, promote, and support excellence in magic and to encourage the development and use of magic for the benefit of mankind. A number of famous and infamous magical experiments were conducted there. It has a reputation for being elitist, and several famous magicians and alchemists have been linked with it, including Sir Isaac Newton.

Seats of Learning: a set of ancient enchanted flying chairs used for getting in and out of the Museum of Magical Miscellany to provide added security and secrecy. Those using the Seats of Learning must drink a

Motion Potion. Each seat is unique and has its own colorful history.

Snook: It's one of the Museum of Magical Miscellany's traditions that new apprentices must bring a magical book—called a Snook—on their first day.

Special Instruction: a binding magical contract, usually an order to do something with a magical object on or by given date. Special Instructions may be placed many years in advance of the designated date. Once received, a Special Instruction may not be canceled. Failure to comply with a magical instruction is against the Lore and may have serious magical repercussions—triggering curses or other unpleasant spells.

Terrible Tomes: the seven most dangerous dark-magic books ever written. They are among the Forbidden Books that must not be opened. It is said that if the Greaders get their hands on just one of the Terrible Tomes, then they could destroy the world.

Unready: people who don't know about magic.

Acknowledgments

This book has been full of surprises. Thanks are due to some very special people who kept me on track and made invaluable contributions.

To my family, especially my sister Lindsay, who lived it with me on all those lunches and walks through the woods. To my son and daughter, Dan and Erin, and my nephew, Harry, who provided encouragement and comments on the many drafts, and grew up while I was busy writing.

To Bryan for being Bryan; and to Ian for always being there when I need him. And to Jane and Charlotte for their support.

To my exceptional agents, Paul Moreton and Eddie

Bell at Bell Lomax Moreton and Josephine Hayes, now at the Blair Partnership, who made it possible in the first place.

To Leah Thaxton, my wonderful publisher at Faber & Faber, and her fantastic team of editors: Alice Swan, Naomi Colthurst, and Natasha Brown.

To Maurice Lyon, who did such a great job copyediting and made many helpful suggestions.

To my brilliant editors at HarperCollins, Antonia Markiet and Abbe Goldberg, who gave their time generously and helped me find my way when I was lost.

To my own Alchemists' Club: the advance readers who helpfully reviewed the early chapters.

To Stuart and Ro for their unwavering friendship.

To Sara, who read the drafts and suffered with me, for her belief and love.

Finally, to my parents, Peter Dearlove and Dorothy Dearlove (née Everest)—for everything.